Mills & Boon
Best Seller Romance

A chance to read and collect some of the best-loved novels from Mills & Boon—the world's largest publisher of romantic fiction.

Every month, four titles by favourite Mills & Boon authors will be re-published in the *Best Seller Romance* series.

A list of other titles in the *Best Seller Romance* series can be found at the end of this book.

Lilian Peake

HEART IN THE SUNLIGHT

MILLS & BOON LIMITED
LONDON · TORONTO

First published 1975
Australian copyright 1982
Philippine copyright 1982
This edition 1982

ISBN 0 263 73826 4

Set in Linotype Plantin 10 on 11pt.
02-0382

Made and printed in Great Britain by
Richard Clay (The Chaucer Press) Ltd,
Bungay, Suffolk

For my daughter Alison, who, like me, remembers Norway with affection.

CHAPTER ONE

'Of all the men in this lounge,' said the tall, fair-haired girl at Noelle's side, 'which one do you think is my brother?'

For a moment, Noelle felt almost too tired to care. She raised a hand and with the back of it pushed from her cheek a stray handful of hair – rich brown hair, which deepened the grey of her eyes. Her body, slim but with a well-defined outline, was bending a little with fatigue and from the weight of the bulging rucksack which was pulling down her shoulders.

The denim jacket she was wearing matched the faded blue of her denim pants, which were creased and splashed here and there with coffee. An awkward passenger in the buffet car on the train had jogged her elbow as she was lifting the cup to her lips. Neither the passenger's profuse apologies nor the numerous paper tissues which she had offered, had been able to wipe away the brown stains.

The journey from Newcastle station to the quay was behind them. The ship's engines – those of the ferry that was taking them across the North Sea to Bergen – had not yet begun to throb, but the inspection of their passports and all the other details connected with travelling to another country had been dealt with.

They had not yet been down to their cabin. Kirsten, Noelle's friend, said she wanted to find her brother. She could have travelled with him in first class comfort, but she had preferred to stay with Noelle, who could not afford to pay for the privilege of travelling with the more prosperous passengers.

Now the two girls stood near the door of the first class lounge. The straps of Noelle's sandals cut into her toes and all she wanted to do was to sit down and rest her tired limbs. But at her friend's bidding she looked around. She supposed it was in her own interests that she identified the man who was to be her employer for the next two or three months.

She eyed the furnishings, the soft, sound-hushing carpet and, most of all, the comfort of the deep armchairs. A man across the lounge lifted his head from the magazine he was reading. He must have caught the longing in Noelle's eyes and misinterpreted it, because the smile that lifted the corners of his mouth had no humour in it, only cynicism and coolness. It contained also the hint of a question.

Noelle's heart bumped and scurried on. What was the man thinking – that she was looking at *him* with longing? His looks were good and he knew it. How many women had been attracted by that honey-gold hair, that touch of icy harshness in the eyes? But even if she was longing for him with all her heart – and that, she assured herself, she was far from doing – she would never let such a man know.

Her eyes, which had been riveted by him, jerked away and continued their search. But her friend was waving and calling across the room in her native Norwegian. And to Noelle's dismay, she seemed to be addressing the man on the other side of the lounge.

Yes, the likeness in their features was unmistakable – the same honey-coloured hair, the same blue eyes, except that Kirsten's were softer. And, as the man drew himself lazily from his chair, there was the similar way of walking. There was little doubt left in Noelle's mind that the man was Kirsten's brother.

Now he was coming towards them and Noelle knew an inexplicable moment of panic. She had to fight an instinctive urge to turn and run. This man was to be her employer through the summer season, and the prospect alarmed her. There was still time, she told herself, despite the administrative barriers through which they had just passed, to catch the first train back to London.

The man was talking, answering his sister as she went forward to greet him. Their brief conversation finished – Noelle had heard her own name mentioned – and the man, his expression a little sardonic, turned his eyes towards her. They wandered over her, narrowing at her appearance, missing nothing – the splashes on her pants, the hair in need of combing, the hand that lifted to the back of her neck, rubbing it to ease away the tension.

'Noelle,' said Kirsten, 'this is my brother, Per, pronounced in your language "Pair". Per, my friend Noelle Roberts.'

Per Arneson formed a smile with his lips, but his eyes, which were fixed on Noelle's face, remaining cool and detached. His hand came out and Noelle, with the barest hesitation – she could not explain even to herself the reason for it – put her hand in his. It was evident from the merest flick of anger that whipped across his eyes that the man who held her hand for only part of a second had not missed it.

Per motioned to a group of chairs round a circular table, and they moved towards them. There were people everywhere. Some seemed agitated at the idea of the nineteen-hour journey in front of them. Others appeared calm and composed as they walked around, or threw themselves into seats, impatient to feel the movement of the ship beneath their feet.

'Please sit down, Miss Roberts, Kirsten.' Per Arneson's English was almost perfect, with only the faintest trace of an accent to colour his tone. He stood while Noelle and Kirsten twisted and shrugged the rucksacks from their shoulders, letting them fall to the floor. Then, when they were seated, he too sat down.

'You have not yet been to your cabin?' he asked.

'We were so anxious to find you, Per,' Kirsten said, laughing.

'We?' Eyebrows rose. 'Miss Roberts, also? I'm flattered indeed that a woman I have not even met should be so eager to make my acquaintance.'

Kirsten laughed again, but Noelle coloured at the sarcasm.

'So, Miss Roberts,' Per went on, 'you are travelling all

this way to work for me at one of my hotels in Norway? For how long – roughly three months?' Noelle nodded. 'You are, like my sister, a student of dress design?'

'No, Herr Arneson,' Noelle replied, her tone barely polite, 'no longer a student. We're both qualified now.' She turned to her friend. 'Kirsten, haven't you told your—'

'Yes, I told my *dear* brother,' Kirsten answered, 'but at times, for reasons unknown to me, he chooses to be obtuse. He knows perfectly well we've passed our exams.' She turned to her brother. 'What is this, Per – an interview? If so, perhaps you would prefer me to be the tactful sister and return to the ladies' cloakroom?'

'My dear Kirsten,' Per Arneson shifted his position, crossed his legs and seemed all set for an entertaining time, 'you cannot expect me to take on to my staff a strange female,' he glanced mockingly at Noelle. 'Forgive the expression, Miss Roberts, but you cannot deny that you are both a stranger and,' his eyes flicked over her, 'female.' He turned again to his sister and continued, 'A strange female without attempting to assess the extent of her intelligence—'

Noelle took exception to the faintly insulting tone. 'My intelligence, Herr Arneson, is surely in little doubt? I have, after all, just passed a series of exams in dress design with honours—'

'You have?' His eyes, as they passed over her again, noting with a touch of distaste her creased, splashed, dishevelled state, held a 'you could have fooled me' expression.

Noelle glanced uncomfortably at her friend. She was dressed in a similar style but had somehow managed to avoid the creases and the travel-worn look that clung, like a layer of tell-tale dust, to Noelle's appearance. Why, Noelle thought, can't I look as cool and calm as Kirsten?

She looked again at Per and found that his eyes had not moved from her. She coloured under his scrutiny and with a combing agitated movement ran her fingers upwards through the back of her hair.

'You think,' their host persisted, 'a qualification – with *honours*,' the emphasis was meant solely to annoy, 'in dress design is a useful asset for someone who is joining the domestic staff of a busy hotel?'

'Stop being difficult, Per,' his sister said. 'Noelle's not one of your employees yet. Until we step inside the door of the Hotel Arneson, she's my friend, and therefore entitled to politeness and reasonable behaviour from my brother.'

'Implying that once she steps inside the door of my hotel, I can treat her impolitely and unreasonably?' He was smiling, but the smile was insincere.

Noelle stirred uncomfortably. Both brother and sister saw the movement and Kirsten said, 'Take no notice of Per, Noelle. He thinks all women are the same.'

'You're wrong, Kirsten. I don't think, I *know* they're the same.' His eyes – those disconcerting blue eyes – came to rest once more on Noelle. 'Where men are concerned, women – all women – are unscrupulous. They search the world – that is, the particular world they live in, their own section of it – for the man who possesses the largest bank balance. Then, having found him, they fasten their claws into him and don't let him go until they have his ring on their finger and his roof over their heads.' He leaned back against the chair, but his eyes, cool and narrow, stayed on Noelle's face. 'I can see by your friend's rather agitated movements, Kirsten, that she does not agree with me. You object to what I'm saying, Miss Roberts?'

'Strongly, Herr Arneson.' She paused to choose her words, but her host interrupted.

'Go on. You're going to say, "If I didn't need the money, if Kirsten were not my friend, I would get up, walk off this ship and catch the next train back home". Am I right?'

Noelle coloured at the accuracy of his guess.

'Ah,' said Per with a smile, 'I'm right. But you do need the money and you are Kirsten's friend, so you're staying. Right again?'

Noelle breathed hard at his arrogance, but she could do

nothing about the angry words which came pouring into her mind. For the next three months she had to be polite to this man, no matter how much he goaded her. But at the end of that time she would give vent to all the stored-up resentment and aggravation and tell him exactly what she thought of him. The idea brought a smile to her face and Per Arneson commented,

'Let us into the secret of your thoughts, Miss Roberts.'

'I'm sorry, Herr Arneson,' she said sweetly. 'When I'm working for you, you may be able to give me orders and exercise control over my physical processes, but under no circumstances will I allow you to exert power over my thought processes. In other words—' dared she say it? She did not need to.

'Mind my own business?' He laughed loudly. 'So you are putting your future employer in his place? Our relationship promises to be a lively one, if nothing else.' He stood, pushing one hand into a pocket and lifting the other to run over his hair. 'Thank you, Kirsten, for bringing your friend. It will be interesting to see how difficult Miss Roberts finds it to curb her rebellion and her spiritedness when she's serving awkward elderly ladies, stubborn old gentlemen and complaining, not to say spoilt, young women, in the course of her work. Because, Miss Roberts,' those eyes were upon her once more, a little cold and a little hard, 'you will have to curb them. I cannot have on my staff a mutinous, insubordinate young woman, no matter how many qualifications she has, *with honours*, if she refuses on principle to take orders from those above her.'

Noelle jerked herself out of the depths of the chair and faced her friend's brother. 'I think, Herr Arneson, it's best if you and I part company here and now.'

She picked up her rucksack, but Per Arneson stepped forward and took it from her, putting it behind him and out of reach.

'You need the money, Miss Roberts, remember?'

There were noises from above and there came the throb of

the engines, setting up vibrations all around. The passengers changed roles. The calm ones became agitated and apprehensive, the restless ones bright-eyed and tranquil. The journey across the North Sea was about to begin.

It was evening. The weather, which had been good all day, was still fine. As Noelle wandered about the deck in a sleeveless top and clean, hip-hugging pants, she did not feel the need of a jacket. The throb beneath her feet was like a rhythmic heartbeat. The ship was steady, with only an occasional dip to one side or the other to remind the passengers that there was water and not land underneath them. The North Sea was behaving itself remarkably well.

Noelle had left Kirsten at the bar, chatting to the young men who had gathered around her. With her good looks, so similar to those of her brother, she had only to glance at a member of the opposite sex and he would move to her side to talk to her.

Noelle wondered if Per Arneson had the same effect on women. No, she told herself, she did not need to wonder. She knew that he did. Short though her acquaintance with him had been, she had felt the strange pull of him herself. Was it, she reflected, those eyes, shrewd, astute, dispassionate and cool? Or the height of him, causing even Noelle, who was a little taller than average, to look up to him? Perhaps it was the breadth of his shoulders, the suggestion of power, leashed but nonetheless perceptible in the way he moved.

She leant against the rail at the stern of the ship and looked down, gazing at the wash which stretched behind them into the far distance. It was possible to trace the path of the vessel. Where it had corrected its course there were long, sweeping curves. The leaping white foam entranced her and she found herself mesmerized by its life and movement.

When Per Arneson joined her at the rail, she did not notice him until he moved. He was near enough to touch as he leaned on his arms beside her. Her pulses beat, erratic and fast, equalling and overtaking the steady throb of the engine. There was nothing steady about her heartbeats. Why this man should, after so short an acquaintance, play such havoc with her feelings was entirely beyond her comprehension. That she had no such effect on his was plain by the slow, lazy smile he turned towards her.

'Fascinating, isn't it?' His white teeth flashed in the darkening evening. 'You can look back all that way and see exactly where the ship has been. It's like looking at the past in the present.' His smile persisted. 'Have you a "past", Miss Roberts? And does it cling to you as the wash clings to this ship?'

What was it he wanted to know? About her private life? He would not hear about it from her. Not that there was anything to hear. 'Yes, I have a past, Herr Arneson. Twenty-two years of it.'

He laughed. 'So you are putting me off. Is it so bad, this "past" of yours, that you will not let me into its secrets? Have you had so many men friends that you have lost count?'

Lost count of the two or three young men who had shown passing interest? Spin-offs, mostly, from Kirsten's magic circle of men. Fellow students at the school of art and design they had both attended, who had been attracted by her quietness, curious to know what might be underneath that calm after Kirsten's clamouring and turbulent attractions.

But they had not stayed long enough to explore her depths. They had touched her long brown hair, looked with interest at her rounded face and desirable figure, put a playful finger on her short, attractive nose, gazed with anticipation at her sensitive mouth – and come up against the cool rebuff in her grey eyes.

Then they had drifted back to Kirsten, who never rebuffed, who gave out encouragement and warmth like a fire on a cold day. Kirsten, who admitted to having too soft a heart where men were concerned. In that, if in nothing else, she differed from her brother. It was necessary, Noelle told herself, only to look into those ice-cold eyes to see that. No soft heart inside that hard, tough body, only a total freedom from reliance on any other human being, whether male or female, for his mental and physical well-being.

'Your silence,' said the man at her side, 'intrigues me. Is there so much to tell that you don't know where to begin?'

Noelle smiled and gazed down at the curling, skipping whiteness of the ship's wash. 'How is it,' she asked, 'that you've lowered yourself to descend to the level of the tourist deck, when you could be enjoying the comforts of the first class lounge?'

He laughed. 'A neat if telling change of subject. Could it not be that I was drawn by the quiet, lonely figure down here, gazing out across the sea? That I wanted to discover why she,' he paused to let his eyes wander over her, 'it was obvious that it was a "she", why,' he repeated, 'she had forsaken her fellow tourists, not to mention my sister, and come out here alone?'

'Your sister, Herr Arneson, hasn't even missed me. She's surrounded by men.'

'You sound just a little sour, Miss Roberts.'

'I'm sorry, I didn't intend to. I'm very fond of your sister. I'm grateful to her for travelling tourist with me when she could have joined you as a first class passenger.'

'You too could have joined me this evening. I invited you both to dine with me in the first class dining-room.'

'It was kind of you,' Noelle lifted her eyes and watched the sun, a great red ball, sink towards the horizon, 'but we preferred to be amongst our contemporaries.'

He winced. 'You hit the target dead centre, Miss Roberts. My extra twelve years weigh heavily upon me.'

'I'm sorry,' she said again. 'I had no intention of hurting. In any case,' she glanced at him, 'your extra years, as you call them, haven't registered at all on your physique.' Then she realized how personal she was getting and coloured.

His laugh rang out. 'You have set my mind at rest. I really began to feel the burden of my thirty-four years.'

Now the sea was darkening as the sun's rays began to diminish. The sun, in setting, lit the sky with a rainbow mixture of yellow-gold and red. It lingered on the horizon as if loath to disappear altogether, and as at last it touched the line dividing the sky and the sea it filled the atmosphere around it with a mass of brilliance. It poured a trail of liquid red across the now black waters as if in a desperate attempt to make its final mark upon the northern hemisphere before sinking into oblivion.

Then it was gone, and Noelle shook herself a little, realizing that she and the man who was still beside her were no longer alone. All around them were people taking pictures of the setting sun.

'Have you returned from your contemplation of the heavens, Miss Roberts?' Per Arneson asked. His voice was soft and without mockery. 'Have you never seen the sun set over the sea before?'

Noelle turned to him. In the darkness the white crispness of the shirt showing beneath his jacket stood out. He had changed for dinner in his first class dining-room.

'Not,' she said, 'from the deck of a ship.'

'You're not a hardened traveller?'

'I've been abroad, but usually by plane.'

'You should come this way more often, then. It's far more restful. I have come across the North Sea many times by ship.' He gazed across the dark waves, now only visible where the reflected lights of the ship danced on them. 'I travel this way because I can unwind better with a deck beneath my feet and the freedom to move or stand still as I please, rather than be confined to one seat in the pressurized cabin of an aircraft.'

'You – unwind, Herr Arneson?'

'So surprised? You think I'm always relaxed, that I never experience tension? That I have no deeper emotions which sometimes get out of hand?' Now he was laughing at her and she was glad of the darkness to hide her confusion.

'I – I think you're always in control. Of people, of

situations, of –'

'Myself?' He supplied the word she was too shy to say. 'Mm, now let me see.' She knew he was smiling in the darkness. 'Yes, I can think of – situations where I throw self-control to the winds and abandon myself entirely to the forces of my emotions. Does that surprise you? Or even shock you?'

'Surprise me? I don't think so. Shock me? No.'

'So you are broadminded in theory?' He was near now, too near for Noelle's peace of mind. 'In practice, too?'

There was a rush of movement behind them and Kirsten said, 'So that is where you are. What are you trying to do, Per – seduce Noelle? Take my word for it, you won't get very far with her. She's so virtuous you wouldn't believe it. I keep telling her her morality is out of date.'

Per turned and leant back with his arms against the rail. In the glow of the lamps which were shining at intervals around the deck, Noelle could see the light of challenge in his eyes. 'You think I wouldn't get far with her if I really tried?' His eyes were narrow now and on Noelle's face, assessing, summing up. 'You want to bet, Kirsten?'

Kirsten's laugh rang out and floated away over the waves. 'I wouldn't waste my money.' She turned away and then back again. 'On second thoughts, Per, I'll take you on. I've always admired your technique, and it would be interesting to see if it's foolproof, or if this is one occasion where it just doesn't work.'

'Kirsten, please!' Noelle appealed. 'How could you let me down . . . '

'You think my sister's throwing you to the wolves, Miss Roberts?'

'Make it singular, Per. Wolf. I have a brother with an insatiable appetite for the opposite sex, Noelle.' Then, softly, thoughtfully, 'I should love to see him go hungry for once.'

They talked for a few minutes in their own language and Noelle, embarrassed, turned to look out over the dark waters. She heard the word *krone* mentioned two or three times. Then Kirsten laughed and shook hands with her brother. It seemed they had made some kind of pact with each other.

Kirsten took Noelle by the arm and pulled her towards the door which led into the lounge. 'There's music and dancing. Come and join in. Leave Per to commune with his first class fellow passengers.'

In the centre was a circular area and, compared with the shadowed lighting of the rest of the lounge, brightly illuminated. On a raised platform a young man was seated at an organ and under his fingers the music swelled and expanded to fill the room and spill out on to the deck, enticing other passengers in. Couples danced and swayed, sometimes colliding in the restricted space.

Subdued though the lighting was, Noelle found herself half closing her eyes after the cool darkness of the deck. As soon as Kirsten stepped through the door she was pulled by a young man to join the dancers.

Noelle, alone now, looked for a seat near a table lamp, picked up a discarded magazine and sat down, flicking through it. A few minutes later a tall, fair-haired young man put himself in front of her and said with a strongly marked accent, 'Dance, please?'

He smiled so sweetly and looked so appealing, Noelle could not bring herself to refuse. As they danced, the young man told her that he was a Norwegian student at an English college and was returning home to Norway for the summer. He had a girl-friend at home, he said, and he was looking forward to seeing her. He also had a girl-friend at the college and he was looking forward to seeing her on his return to England. Noelle laughed with him and he said, 'Now I have a girl-friend on this ship, have I not?'

Noelle shook her head and said gently, 'I'm with a friend and – and her brother.'

'And this brother, he is your boy-friend?'

'No! He's – he's – ' What could she say? 'He's old, much too old.'

'Fifty, perhaps?'

'No, no. He's thirty-four.' Then her heart nearly stopped as she caught sight of a familiar figure standing just within the circle of light and watching the dancers. His face was cold, his eyes were colder. He must have overheard what she had said. She had meant it as a joke, but it was obvious that Per Arneson regarded it as a bad joke.

The music stopped and Noelle slipped away as another girl claimed the young man's attention. Noelle was on the opposite side of the circle from where Per Arneson was standing and she melted into the dimness of the lounge, mingling with the other passengers and finding a seat which was so far removed from a light that it was in almost total darkness.

She would not be able to read, but that did not matter. She would be hidden from Kirsten's brother and that, at the moment, was all that mattered. She closed her eyes, thinking a little childishly that the action would make her invisible to him – if, indeed, he was even looking for her. The organ played, the passengers laughed, now and then the ship swayed slightly, reminding them that beneath them was not land but water, fathoms deep. The waves lifted and fell, the sea moved restlessly, bearing the ship relentlessly, inexorably towards the end of its journey. And all the time there was the throb of the engines.

A strange sensation prickled Noelle's skin. Her eyes came open to find that only an arm's length away, and lounging against the wall, was the man from whom she had been trying to hide.

But he was not looking at her. He did not even seem to be aware of her presence. Irrationally she grew annoyed at being so ignored, and felt the urge to do something, anything to attract his attention. Her eyes lifted and sought his face. It was serious and he seemed absorbed in his thoughts. A lamp nearby highlighted the fairness of his hair and the resolution in his strong features.

With the arrogant lift of his head, surely inherited from

his Viking ancestors, he looked what he was – successful businessman and wealthy owner of a group of thriving hotels. It was in the cut of his clothes, his ease of manner and his extreme, and slightly intimidating, self-sufficiency.

He continued to treat her as if she was not there, but Noelle's pride refused to behave with the kind of studied contempt Per Arneson was handing out to her. She was not an employee of his yet. She was at that moment his equal socially if not in status or financial standing. It was his air of supreme detachment from his surroundings, his complete self-mastery, no matter what the circumstances, that irritated Noelle to the point of rashness.

She said, raising her voice over the sound of the music and bridging the small gap between them, 'Why have you joined the tourist class passengers, Herr Arneson, when you could be lounging in first-class luxury amongst your equals? Curious, perhaps, as to how the less privileged, the lower levels of society manage, against all odds, to enjoy themselves?'

Slowly Per Arneson's head turned. His eyes, below freezing, came to rest on hers. Involuntarily a shudder went through her. 'I may be a rich man, Miss Roberts,' he said icily, 'but I'm neither insensitive, blind nor deaf. I see, I hear, I feel for those less fortunate than myself. I give generously to charity, I even help actively sometimes. You, for instance – by giving you a job for which you are neither qualified, nor as far as I can judge as a result of my short acquaintance with you, temperamentally suited. But you are my sister's friend. I don't want to let my sister down, so I employ you on the staff of one of my hotels.'

'Thanks,' said Noelle, scarlet now although admitting secretly that she had asked for it, 'for your *charity*. But you can keep it.'

She shot to her feet, but before she could take a step his hand came out and restrained her.

'There's nowhere to run, Miss Roberts. If you stepped off

this ship you would have a long, long way to swim back to your homeland.'

'Hey, little girl!' The tall young Norwegian had found her again. 'Come, my girl-friend of the voyage. Dance with me.'

Noelle shook Per's hand from her arm, gave the young man a brilliant smile and let him lead her back to the dancers.

Breakfast was behind them when it was announced over the ship's loudspeaker system that land had been sighted. There was a rush to the sides of the ship. Binoculars were lifted to eager eyes, telescopic lenses were fitted into place, shutters clicked, ciné cameras whirred. All the same, it took a long time for that land to come within the range of the naked eye.

Noelle had not seen Per Arneson that morning until the moment of the announcement, then he appeared among a group of people on the upper deck. There was a small gate across the top of the stairway leading to the deck which carried the words, 'First Class Passengers only'. Those words placed Per Arneson in a different world.

Now he gazed down at Noelle with a sardonic smile. He leant forward on his arms against the white-painted rail and lifted his hand in a careless salute.

Kirsten cupped her hands and shouted, 'Come down here amongst the poor and underprivileged.' But her brother merely smiled and lifted his head to gaze narrowly in the direction of his homeland.

It was when the ship was feeling its way – its speed had been reduced considerably – between the multitude of rocky islands which were scattered round the waters on the approach to Bergen, that Noelle felt the pressure of another passenger beside her. There were people everywhere, so she did not at first take much notice, but when she turned her head at last, she saw that Per Arneson had in fact taken his sister's advice and come amongst the 'poor and underprivileged.'

Noelle did not speak, nor did Per. In the background,

Kirsten's laughter came bubbling up from the chatter of passengers. Per Arneson's arm was pressed against Noelle's, his shoulder against her shoulder, and he wished agitatedly that there was not such a crush of people so eager to watch the beauties of Norway's coastline that the man beside her had to stand so near. That he did not seem to mind, or even to notice, was evident in his face. It was serious and gazed with pleasure and a kind of contentment across the calm waters towards his own country.

The mountains rose, it seemed, straight from the sea. Behind them were more mountains and behind those even more, range upon range, fading at last into mist. The lower slopes were tree-covered, the higher sheer and daunting, even against the blueness of the sky. Climbing all over the lower hills were houses, in groups, in rows or perched adventurously and alone away from their fellows. Red-slated roofs, white-walled houses, hotels painted yellow, spires painted blue, all caught the rays of the sun and reflected them back as if determined to share as well as absorb their warmth and light.

'You're pleased with your first sight of my country, Miss Roberts?' Per Arneson's voice spoke softly at her side.

He talks, Noelle thought abstractedly, as a man might talk of a beloved wife, as if his country were part of himself. What would it be like, she found herself wondering, if he ever spoke of a woman with such affection, such – love? And what would it be like, came the whisper of a question, to be that woman he admired and respected so much?

She did not even try to find the answer, because there was no answer. A man with a head as cool as this man's could not possibly possess the warmth and the passion which was an indispensable ingredient of such intense feeling. He could love his country because it would ask nothing of him. He could not love a woman because of the involvement and unselfishness and self-commitment it would entail.

'It's beautiful,' she replied, and gestured with her hands. 'All those islands with their sea birds and the lonely cottages on the edge of the rocks, and,' turning towards the mainland, 'those mountains—' She shook her head, lost for words.

He seemed content with her reply. 'Wait until you see the fjords,' he commented. They stood in silence until he said, 'You may not know that Bergen dates from around 1070 and is Norway's second largest town. If you had more time, if,' he turned his head and smiled mockingly, 'you were not on your way to a life of slavery under the roof of one of my hotels, you could have toured the town. There's a great deal to see. For instance, Edvard Grieg's home, the historical and maritime museums, the aerial cableway to Mount Ulriken, and so on.'

'I'll have to come here some time for a *holiday*,' she said, smiling.

He smiled back and her heart jerked restlessly. His smile illuminated his face much as the sun shining on the walls and windows of the buildings revealed unexpected elements of life and promise which would have stayed in hiding had the buildings remained in shadow.

Noelle pulled herself together. A smile from this man – wordly, knowledgeable, with his *appetite*, as his sister had put it, for women – and her pulses raced and tumbled over each other like waves meeting the shore?

'Little girl, hey there!' Her friend of the evening before elbowed his way through the crush of passengers and made a place for himself on Noelle's other side. 'You must tell me your name and where you will be staying. I have found you and will not let you go out of my life.'

Noelle laughed at his dramatic tone and the hand on his heart. 'I'm sorry,' she answered, 'but I've come to Norway to work, not to play.' Where would she be working? he asked. A long way from here, she told him.

'If it is the other end of Norway, I will come and see you.'

'At the—' She glanced to her left, but her future employer's eyes were fixed on the mountains behind Bergen. 'At the Hotel Arneson, Vulavik. But I'm sorry, I shall be busy. I've come to work, to earn money—'

'But you will have free time? You will not have a boss, I hope, who treats you like a slave—'

Noelle said quickly, 'My – my boss is here. Herr Arneson, Herr Per Arneson.' Per inclined his head, his eyes cold.

But the young man was not put off by Per's distant manner. 'Herr Arneson, I have heard of you, of your excellent hotels. You will give my new friend time off, you will not keep her chained to her job?'

'We're in the twentieth century,' Per drawled. 'I treat my employees with humanity and respect their freedom and —' Per's eyes rested momentarily on Noelle, 'their persons, provided they deserve that respect.' He finished shortly, turning back to the view, 'She will have time off.'

'Then,' said the young man triumphantly, 'I shall ring you—' He leaned forward and spoke to Per, 'She will be allowed phone calls?' Per nodded curtly. 'Good. And I shall call on you.'

'But you told me,' Noelle said, laughing, 'you have girl-friends already. One in England, one in Norway—'

'You have boy-friends in Norway?' His eyebrows went up endearingly. 'No? Then I shall be your boy-friend in Norway.' He found his diary. 'Your name?' Noelle told him.

'But I don't know your name,' she added.

'It is Einar, Einar Olsen. I come from northern Norway, but I shall be visiting an aunt in Bergen for a few weeks before returning home.' The young man saw a friend across the deck, raised his hand and shouted, 'I am coming!' To Noelle he said, 'I shall not forget you, Noelle.' His arms closed round her in a bear-hug, his lips pressed against her cheek and he sighed. 'Ah, this is excellent. You do me good already. *Adjö*,' he whispered, '*på gjensyn*. I'll see you again.'

When he had gone, Noelle turned to Per. 'I'm sorry. I tried not to encourage him, but—'

'So I noticed,' Per answered dryly. 'You put up some very pretty token resistance – which of course made him all the keener.'

Noelle turned on him, forgetting for the moment that this man was her future employer. 'You're quite wrong,' she exclaimed. 'My mind isn't as devious as that.'

The eyebrows rose, whether in reprimand or surprise, Noelle did not bother to work out. 'No? You would hardly be a woman, Miss Roberts, if you did not think one thing and act another.'

'Which proves how little you know about women.'

'Forgive me for disagreeing with you. I know a great deal about women. A man in my position, with money, with – comparative – youth and, like myself, no ties, has early in his adulthood to make his choice. Either he turns and runs from the opposite sex, or he goes towards them as they pursue him with their arms outstretched.'

Noelle refused to ask the question she knew he intended her to ask. He answered it for her, all the same.

'I go towards them. After all, I'm a man, and although you will not believe it, made of flesh and blood.' He studied her face. 'I know what you're thinking. "I am one woman who will not run towards Per Arneson, arms outstretched". Am I right?'

'Yes,' she replied stiffly.

He smiled slightly and murmured, 'Well, we shall see.'

She jerked from his side, said, 'Please excuse me, I'm going to find Kirsten,' and left him.

The less, she thought furiously, I have to do with that man, the better I shall like it. If it wasn't for Kirsten, and if she didn't need the money Per Arneson was going to pay her, she would step ashore at Bergen and board the next ship home. But – and it was that 'but' which carried her, without looking back, and with Kirsten at her side – Per Arneson had business to attend to in Bergen – all the way to Voss by train and all the way by coach from Voss to Vulavik.

When they arrived in the forecourt of the Hotel Arneson, they saw Per's car standing near the entrance. He had arrived before them after all.

CHAPTER TWO

THE hotel was built near the edge of a fjord. It was a long, low building, in three sections, each of them two storeys high and linked by walk-ways.

Noelle and Kirsten climbed down the steps of the coach and hoisted their rucksacks on to their backs.

'I'm hot and thirsty,' Kirsten announced as they walked towards the entrance, 'and so are you. First we will shower, then we will order tea.'

With some misgiving, Noelle followed her friend through the swing doors into the hotel entrance foyer. 'But, Kirsten, I've come to work. I'm not on holiday.'

'We've been travelling since early yesterday,' Kirsten answered. 'No one, not even my brother, could expect you to start work without a break.'

She spoke in Norwegian to the girl behind the reception desk. The girl, recognizing Kirsten, smiled and turned to a row of hooks behind her. She gave Kirsten a key. They exchanged a few more words of greeting, then over her shoulder Kirsten said, 'Follow me, Noelle.'

As they walked side by side along a corridor, Kirsten said, 'Whenever I stay here I live in Per's apartment. There are two bedrooms, so I have the spare one. The staff live in a house across the road. Per has a room in it in case of emergencies. Needless to say, it's better fitted out than all the other rooms. He has all the modern amenities, plus, plus.'

They stopped in front of a door which seemed to be the only one along the entire length of the corridor. As they entered the apartment, Noelle caught her breath. The living room was carpeted from wall to wall in white, the outer wall consisting only of windows, double glazed for warmth, Kirsten explained. The room as a whole had an uncluttered air, the few pieces of furniture it contained being modern in design and function. The curtains were floor-length and blue, echoing in colour the rugs which were scattered here and there.

To the left, Kirsten explained, was a large kitchen. To the right were the two bedrooms. Each bedroom had a bathroom attached.

'This is mine,' Kirsten called over her shoulder, turning into a doorway which opened off the living area. She shrugged herself from under the rucksack and flung it down, inviting Noelle to do the same. 'Make yourself at home.' She gestured towards a door which led out of the bedroom. 'Take a shower. There are plenty of towels in there.'

But Noelle frowned. 'I couldn't, Kirsten. I'm here to work, not to—'

'Noelle, *min kjære venninne*, my dear friend, you have said that before. You're boring me. What are you afraid of?'

'Your brother might—'

'My brother? You are afraid of my brother?'

'What are *you* doing here?' The voice came from behind them. The two girls turned, Kirsten smiling, Noelle with a curious kind of foreboding. Yes, he had been addressing her, not his sister.

'You came in quietly, Per. Next time make more noise. As you probably heard, Noelle is afraid of you!'

But Per did not seem to be listening to his sister's chatter. Still looking at Noelle, he repeated, a little more coldly, if that were possible, 'What are you doing here?'

'I – I—' Noelle looked helplessly at Kirsten.

'I brought her. Why shouldn't I?'

Per answered in Norwegian, then stopped and turned to Noelle with a mocking bow. 'Excuse me, Miss Roberts. For a moment I forgot your presence. I must talk in your language. It is essential that you feel at *home.*' The emphasis was derisive, implying that she had no right to feel at home in her employer's apartment.

He turned again to Kirsten. 'Why did you not take her to

Roy Vikör, the assistant *direktör*? He would have directed her to the staff quarters.'

'She's my friend, Per.'

'She is first and foremost a member of my domestic staff. I believe,' to Noelle, 'that is the whole object of this visit of yours to my hotel?'

'Per, stop being so unpleasant. Her duties haven't begun yet.'

'They began, as with all the other girls who start today, as soon as she set foot inside the entrance foyer. She's not a guest.'

'She's my friend, Per,' Kirsten repeated, 'and as such has free access to my room.'

'*Min kjære söster*,' he drawled, 'you brought her here – to work for me. It was at your suggestion, you told me, that she crossed the North Sea and had a working holiday.'

Scarlet-faced, Noelle shouldered her rucksack and went to the door. Kirsten said, 'Noelle, come back! Don't let my brother's lack of manners drive you away.'

'Lack of *manners*?' Her brother turned on her. 'You accuse *me* of that when it was you who broke the rules by bringing her here?'

'I allowed myself to be brought here, Herr Arneson, so surely it was I who broke the rules?'

'My sister is quite capable of defending herself, Miss Roberts. There's no need for you to do it for her.'

Pale now and on the verge of tears, Noelle said, 'Kirsten, where do I go?'

'I'll take you,' Per said curtly. 'If Kirsten takes you, you'll probably finish up in the dining-room being waited on by the guests. Come with me. I shall show you to your room.'

'I hope you realize,' Kirsten called after them, 'how honoured you are, Noelle, having the top man, the *direktör* himself, take you to the staff quarters. You are making history. I assure you, it has never been heard of before.'

As they walked out into the corridor, Noelle said stiffly, 'I'm sorry to cause you all this trouble, Herr Arneson. In the next three months I shall do my best to remember my place.'

He stopped in his tracks and faced her. In his anger his fingers twitched and in that moment he looked capable of doing her an injury.

Noelle realized how provocatively she had spoken to the top man, as his sister had called him, the owner himself, and apologized again, sincerely this time.

He did not seem greatly mollified by her words. 'I must admit to being seriously worried, Miss Roberts. In fact, if you were not a friend of Kirsten's, I would, at this point, have told you I did not consider you were made of the right material for a member of my domestic staff, and asked you to go. How can I be sure you will keep your temper with the guests – and some of them can be extremely trying – if you cannot keep it with me?'

She wanted to tell him. But there's something about you that arouses me almost to a state of fury. That was what it was, wasn't it, this feeling she got whenever he came near, even when he came into the same room?

But she could not, of course, say the words which were in her mind. She could only stand there staring at the floor and biting her lip in an effort to keep it still.

'Come,' he said, after a few moments during which he had stared at her bent head, 'follow me.'

Curious glances came their way as they swept across the entrance foyer to the door. Per was moving so fast Noelle found it a strain keeping up with him. Her rucksack seemed to be growing heavier with every step, but Per remained completely unconcerned by her faint gasps as she walked beside him.

They crossed the road – despite the fact that Vulavik was a village, it seemed to be a busy place – and climbed a slope to the front door of a three-storeyed wooden house. There seemed, to Noelle's confused eyes, to be a large number of people moving around the house, girls, women, young men. Everyone stared as they climbed the stairs to the first floor.

Per looked at the numbers on the doors and opened one, having knocked first and received no reply. It was a large room and there were three beds in it. Hiding her dismay – she told herself she was a fool to think she would have a room to herself – Noelle walked in.

She could not have hidden her disappointment very well, because Per said, 'What's the matter? Isn't it good enough for my sister's friend?'

Noelle was about to respond angrily to the hidden accusation that she considered herself above the other members of staff, but bit her lip in time. She must not be accused again of impoliteness, because she knew for certain it would be for the last time. Per Arneson would not reprimand an employee more than once for lack of control over her tongue. He would show her the door and expect her to pass through it, out of his hotel – and his life.

She opted for silence because she could not really tell him what was troubling her. It was impossible to explain to such a man – whose emotions obviously never got the better of him – that she found it difficult to sleep in a room where other people were also sleeping. It was foolish of her to have been unprepared for the necessity of sharing a room.

He was still looking at her with a deep frown, so Noelle said, 'Thank you for taking the trouble to show me the way, Herr Arneson.' If he thought she was dismissing him, then he would be right.

He lifted his eyebrows, gave a brief, slightly derisive bow and left her.

The room was long and rather narrow. Against one wall were three beds and each bed was divided from the other by a bedside cabinet. The tables beside two of the beds were cluttered with personal belongings, a shaded lamp and a ticking alarm clock. Noelle looked closely at one of them and saw that it was set for a dauntingly early six o'clock, almost two hours earlier than she had set hers to go off while a student at the college and living in a rented room.

The time on one of the alarm clocks told her that it was just past four in the afternoon, and she became aware of how thirsty she was. She wished she had been allowed by the *direktör* to share the tea his sister had been intending to send for.

She was wandering restlessly round the room wondering what to do, when there was a tap on the door and a woman walked in. The woman was well-built and middle-aged, her once fair hair now turning grey.

'You are Fröken Roberts?' she asked, holding out her hand and speaking in careful English. 'I am Fru Vatne, the *oldfrue*, the housekeeper. Herr Arneson has told me you were here and I am to outline your duties. He also instructed me to provide you with food if you require it.'

The owner's surprising attentiveness made Noelle colour a little. 'That was very kind of him,' she murmured.

'You are a family friend, he explained. Is that not so?'

'A friend of his sister's, yes, but—'

'That would explain his attention to your case. It is very unusual for the *direktör* to concern himself with the personal affairs of the domestic staff. Now, you would like some food? And some tea, perhaps?' She smiled and Noelle warmed to her.

'Please, Fru Vatne.'

'I will order it now from the kitchen, and then come back and tell you what you will be doing.'

Fru Vatne soon returned, saying that the tea would not be long. 'Later,' she told Noelle, 'you will be provided with a dress which is the hotel uniform. Soon you, together with some other girls who arrived today, will be given training by the head waiter on the art of waiting at table. After that, you will be free for the remainder of the evening.'

When the tea arrived, the housekeeper left, saying that she hoped Noelle would be happy for the duration of her stay at the Hotel Arneson.

Noelle had finished the tea and sandwiches and was wondering what to do about the tray when two girls burst into the room and came to a stop at the sight of her.

They were black-haired and animated and one of them said in English, but with a heavy accent, 'Hi. You are English? You look it. You are the new one we were expecting? We are Maria and Sophia and we come from Italy. You are a student, like us?'

'I was,' Noelle told them. 'I've just qualified – in dress design.'

They made appreciative exclamations and looked down ruefully at their old denim pants and open-necked shirts. 'You must excuse us. We have been off duty. Now we have returned to clean ourselves and dress to go back on duty. Excuse us, please.'

They rummaged in the wardrobe and pulled out two tangerine-coloured dresses with touches of white at the neck, waist and skirt. The two girls made faces at the garments, but Noelle thought them attractive, having expected the hotel uniform to be the usual unimaginative black and white. 'You will get one like this,' they told her. 'With your brown hair, it should suit you.'

Then they forgot about her and chattered to each other in their own language. Noelle felt cut off and lonely. She wished she could go across to the hotel and find Kirsten. But she knew where Kirsten would be – in her brother's apartment, and that, to a lowly waitress, would from now on be forbidden territory. Hadn't the owner himself made that perfectly clear?

Maria saw the tray. 'You have been given tea? Up here?' Noelle nodded, feeling for some reason guilty. 'You did not have to go downstairs to the staff dining-room?'

'I didn't know there was a staff dining-room,' Noelle said. 'The housekeeper came to see me because Herr Arneson told her to—'

'*Herr Arneson* told her?' The girls looked at Noelle with new interest. 'You know him well, the owner? You are his—' They looked at each other and smiled. 'You are his – friend?'

The pause before the final word gave it a deeper meaning. Noelle shook her head uncomfortably and Sophia went on, 'Why be so scared of us knowing? It goes on all the time here. We also have boy-friends. Ah, Norwegian men . . .' They clasped their hands and turned up their eyes.

Had the owner of Hotel Arneson such a reputation, and amongst his own staff?

'I'm a friend of his sister's,' Noelle explained, and the girls laughed, not really believing her.

Later, Noelle met the other girls who had arrived that day. Their backgrounds and nationalities were varied. One or two came from Iceland, another from Canada, yet another from Denmark. They were all students, and all were there to earn money for their own personal reasons.

They were introduced by the housekeeper, Fru Vatne, to the head waiter.

'My name is Olaf Krüger,' he said, 'and I am the *hovmester,* the head waiter. You have come here to be waitresses, and I wish to give you a little tuition in the approved method of waiting on the guests at table. In Norway,' he smoothed back the small pieces of hair that remained on his head, 'a feature of our way of life is the "cold table", the *smörgåsbord,* where a large number of appetizing and nutritious foods are set out and to which the guests help themselves.'

He looked round. 'As you will understand, this is a form of self-service and you will be required to stand in the background, being available whenever your help or guidance is needed. But at this hotel we are a little different. We serve dinner in the evening to the guests at their tables. Now for this purpose you will need some teaching in how to serve them with their food without,' he smiled, 'tipping the contents of the dishes into their laps or down their backs!' His audience laughed. He held up his hand. 'I can assure you, it is no laughing matter. But take heart, it has never happened in this hotel yet.'

'It's the custom,' he said, 'to serve guests on their left and collect the empty plates – always,' his eyes twinkled, 'we hope their plates are empty – from the right. However, do not be alarmed if you forget this rule sometimes. People prefer these days less formality and like to see moving around the tables attractively dressed young women with life, energy and smiling faces. They, especially the men, will forgive you a great deal – even a helping of potato in their laps – if it is deposited there by a bright, pretty young lady!'

When the laughter had died down, he continued, 'However, there are some things you must do, some rules you must observe,' and he went on to tell them these rules in detail. It was tiring work, he said, and it might take them time to get used to being on their feet for so long. He advised them to wear comfortable shoes and always, he said, they must have clean hands.

When Noelle dispersed with the others, she felt just a little less apprehensive about the work she had travelled so far to do.

Her two room-mates went off to meet their boy-friends, leaving Noelle wondering how to pass the rest of the evening. Was it permissible for her, now she was an employee, to go across the road into the hotel and look for Kirsten? If she met Kirsten's autocratic brother, would he – verbally – take her by the collar and march her out?

As Fru Vatne had promised, the tangerine-coloured dress which constituted the hotel uniform was waiting for her on her bed. She tried it on and it fitted her surprisingly well. Fru Vatne, she decided, must have good judgment where measurements were concerned. She hung the dress in the wardrobe, then looked ruefully at the denim pants which had been splashed with coffee on the train. They would have to be washed before she could wear them again. There was another pair in her rucksack and these she drew out, shaking them free of creases.

With her matching denim jacket swinging loosely round her shoulders, she crossed the road. She hesitated momentarily outside the hotel entrance, wondering if she ought to find the staff entrance and use that instead, then she pushed boldly against the glass swing doors.

Inside was air-conditioned coolness, floor-standing vases with tall flowers and tapering leaves. People, replete with after-dinner fullness, lounged in chairs, magazines or newspapers held high as they stretched out their legs.

It would be pleasant, Noelle thought, trying vainly to suppress a rush of longing, to be a guest in this hotel, to be waited on, to be the *equal* of Per Arneson, instead of one of his subordinates. To be at the receiving end of his solicitude, his concern for her welfare as a patron of his hotel . . .

With a jerk, she came to her senses. She was here to work, not to enjoy herself. She was here because she was the friend of Kirsten Arneson, sister of the owner. She doubted very much whether that owner would have taken her on to his staff had she not been his sister's friend.

She walked quickly across the foyer and opened the door to the bar. As she had guessed, Kirsten was there, surrounded by men. Kirsten saw her and made frantic 'come and join us' gestures, but although Noelle lifted her hand in recognition, she shook her head, smiled and withdrew. Instead of pushing herself in where she plainly was not expected, she decided to take a walk outside. Surely as an employee she was allowed to breathe the air around the hotel, if not inside it?

The fjord was so near it took only a few moments to reach it. It lapped at Noelle's feet against the concrete base of the promenade. A few steps behind her was the long, paved walk which bordered the hotel. On to this walk opened doors from the bedrooms, which meant that in good weather guests could change in their rooms and run out barefoot to swim in the open-air pool – heated, the brochure said – and which rippled and sparkled in the evening sun. Nearby the Norwegian flag fluttered proudly from a flag pole.

On the fjord itself, anchored near to the embankment, were two or three motor boats and rowing boats, bearing the words 'Hotel Arneson'. Around the pool there were chairs, empty now because the declining sun had lost much of its warmth.

But it was the view which drew Noelle's eyes. Across the fjord were hills, tree-covered and scattered with houses, some forming small villages, others placed high above them. Behind these hills were higher hills, and these in turn were dwarfed by mountains. On the mountain summits snow still lay, and the deep ravines, reluctant to have their secrets revealed, caught and shadowed the sun's rays even when the rest of the mountain was bathed in gold. Racing from summit to valley was a waterfall, appearing from that distance to be a long, thin line of foam hurling down to meet the next fjord, which was hidden from sight.

Noelle turned and scanned the hotel from one end to the other. It had obviously been added to at various times, since it spread out, long and low, bounded on one side by the fjord and on the other by the road.

Her eyes were drawn involuntarily to the central building. With a shock she realized she was staring straight at the owner's apartment. At the window, the owner himself was watching her. Even from that distance she sensed that his eyes held a hint of reprimand. Was he silently rebuking her for trying, in her imagination, to enjoy – without paying – some of the amenities, not to mention the beauties, so readily available to the guests?

Noelle met his gaze with defiance, turning away with an indignant toss of her head. She thrust her hands into her jacket pockets and stared at the rippling water in front of her. Perhaps if she pretended the owner was not there . . .

'Hi there!' Her head swung round to find a young man approaching. He was brown-haired, as casually dressed as herself, and he wore spectacles which gave him a slightly learned air. 'Mark Anderson, from England. Who are you?' Noelle told him. 'Working here, like me?' he asked.

Noelle nodded. 'Waiting at table. I start tomorrow. What do you do?'

He laughed. 'Wash the dishes.' When Noelle said she didn't believe him, he said, 'It's a fact. I'm what could be regarded as casual labour. I came to Norway for my summer vacation, searched in my pocket for enough money to pay for a night at the hotel and found I was running short of cash. So I knocked on the back door, asked if they had a job for me and they said yes, they wanted a dishwasher – on two legs, not the mechanical variety. So here I am, for an indefinite length of time.'

Noelle tried to place him and he must have felt her scrutiny because he said, 'You a student, like me?'

She explained that her college days were behind her because she had just qualified. 'When I go back home I'll get a job.'

Mark explained that he was a third year economics student. 'After this,' he said, 'do you reckon I'd qualify to become a *home* economics student?'

They laughed together and he motioned towards the road which led uphill. 'Care to join me in a walk?'

As they turned towards the road, Noelle gave a hurried, if strangely guilty glance towards the owner's apartment. Yes, he was still there, but his stare had turned cynical, the smile which curved his lips mocking.

Why was the man smiling like that? Wasn't she, Noelle asked herself angrily, proving him wrong? Wasn't she showing him that she was one woman who did not spend her time looking for the richest man of her acquaintance and losing no time in 'getting her claws into him' as he had so derisively put it? Wasn't she also showing him that she was one woman who did not 'run towards' Per Arneson with her 'arms outstretched'?

For a few seconds she lingered, turning towards him and letting him see the anger and the defiance in her face, then she ran to join her companion.

That night Noelle was in bed when her room-mates returned. They were not alone. Outside the door they stood whispering and Noelle could hear the sound of men's voices. The door opened and one of the girls said, 'It is no use. *She* is in there. She has gone to bed already.'

One of the men protested and the girl said, 'You cannot come in tonight.' There followed a series of giggles, then, 'Go, go. You will have to accept your disappointment. She's a spoilsport, that girl.'

Noelle had no doubt that they were referring to her. The two girls came in and the room was flooded with light. Noelle dipped her head under the bedclothes. Maria said, her voice falsely apologetic,

'Oh, you were asleep? We are so sorry. But now you are awake, we can talk, Sophia and I. You do not mind, Noelle?'

Slow, a little dazedly, Noelle shook her head. What else, in the circumstances, could she do? They talked so loudly, now and then breaking into song, and took so long preparing themselves for bed, even slipping out to have a shower, that Noelle gave up trying even to rest. She pulled a sweater over her nightdress, found a paperback and tried to lose herself in its pages.

Even when, at past midnight, the girls turned out the light, they did not stop talking. This was something Noelle had dreaded. She had never found it easy to sleep in the same room as a friend, let alone two girls who were complete strangers – and noisy ones at that.

When at last they were quiet, Noelle found herself wide awake, and it was not until dawn began to colour the mountains that she fell asleep.

When the alarm clocks rang, setting up a clamouring vibration in Noelle's over-sensitive ears, she moaned and clapped her pillow round her head. Maria and Sophia threw back the covers and slid out of bed. Noelle envied them their energy. Her first day on duty and she felt as worn out as if she had been on her feet all night!

Maria came over and tugged the bedclothes to the bottom of the bed. 'Up, up, you must get up,' she sang, then repeated it in Italian. 'We must wash, dress and eat before we start work. And breakfasts for the hotel guests are served from seven o'clock.'

Noelle washed and slipped into her uniform, combing her hair and leaving it to hang loosely, framing her face. As she applied a little make-up she thought, It's lucky my disturbed night doesn't show in my face. As long as my energy holds out . . . But she knew that the excitement which was bubbling inside her like a sparkling wine would carry her through to the end of the day.

It was not until after lunch that Noelle found herself free again. Part of her duties had been to help to arrange the *smörgåsbord* – the cold table – with the foods the cook had prepared. There had been salads, cold meats and fish; tomatoes, slices of goat's cheese, both white and brown; sardines and pilchards in tins. 'Leave the food alone,' the head waiter had told them, 'to speak for itself.'

There had been hot dishes for lunch, too, with sausages and omelettes and hot vegetables. Guests helped themselves and many of them had returned for more. Noelle, with the other waitresses, had been told to stand ready to give help and advice. Then, when lunch was over, they had cleared the tables.

Noelle saw Mark Anderson in the kitchens. He had a large apron round his waist and there were two or three other young men washing and drying the dishes. They joked and laughed, mostly in English, because it seemed that most of them, whatever their nationality, spoke the language, even if only haltingly. Noelle felt guilty because her ability to speak other languages lagged so far behind theirs.

Noelle met Kirsten on her way to the staff house. 'When you've changed,' Kirsten said, 'come to Per's place.'

'But, Kirsten, I'm an employee now. I can't keep wishing myself on your brother—'

'Per's in the office, so you can stop worrying about him.'

But when Noelle stepped inside the large, cool lounge

that belonged to her employer, she looked round quickly, feeling he was there looking at her as he had looked last evening when she had stood at the water's edge. It was imagination, however, because it was Kirsten who had let her in and she was alone.

Spread over the white carpet were pieces of a pattern cut out of newspaper. 'I'm designing myself a dress,' Kirsten said. 'Tell me what you think of it.'

For some time they discussed the technicalities of the pattern and its style. Kirsten mixed them each a drink.

'Won't your brother mind?' Noelle asked, afraid that any moment the owner might walk in.

Kirsten shrugged. 'Too bad if he does. He can easily replace what we're drinking. He's got so much money he doesn't really know what to do with it. A lot of it, of course, he ploughs back into the business – building extensions to his hotels, modernizing the equipment, replacing worn furniture. But he knows how to spend it in other ways, too. He goes skiing in the winter, in the summer he sails a yacht. He owns two or three cars, all fast, all expensive. If he was not my brother, and if I didn't know he worked so hard, I might be tempted to call him the playboy type.'

'Women?' asked Noelle, her throat a little tight.

'Women! They swarm round him, and he brushes them off – those he doesn't want – like flies.'

'Those he does want?' Even as she spoke, Noelle reproached herself for the question.

Kirsten laughed. 'I leave that to your imagination!'

'Leave what to her imagination?' The words were drawled from the door.

Noelle uncurled herself from the stroke-soft pile of the carpet and stood to face Kirsten's brother. Her cheeks were scarlet, her hands moist. Would he throw her out?

Kirsten answered blandly, quite unmoved by her brother's sudden appearance, 'What you do with the women you want.'

Per looked Noelle over. 'If your friend's morals are as

pure as you say they are, she hasn't very much to go on, has she? You – er – enjoyed your walk with your newfound boy-friend, Miss Roberts? You – walked – far into the night?' He looked at her narrowly.

Noelle knew that he had not missed her shadowed eyes – as the hours had passed so her tiredness had increased – and felt a swift, angry resentment at his interpretation of their meaning.

Kirsten looked up from her pattern. 'Boy-friend? Noelle?'

'Why are you so surprised?' her brother asked. 'She seems to find it as easy as a marksman picking off a moving target. On the ship it was one of our countrymen. Beside the fjord it was one of her own.'

'It must be the Norwegian air,' Kirsten said, smiling. 'In England she seemed to frighten them away. Or drive them away.' She looked at Noelle. 'I never could quite decide which.'

Per's cool eyes fastened on to Noelle again. 'You didn't answer my question, Miss Roberts.'

So he was not going to let the subject drop? Noelle told herself that she knew why. He wanted to prove to his sister how wrong she was about her friend's morals.

'I may be on your payroll, Herr Arneson,' she answered tartly, 'but you don't pay me to tell you about my private life.'

Kirsten burst out laughing and clapped her hands. 'Oh, good, good!'

Per's eyes slitted. 'It would *pay* you, Miss Roberts, to be a little more amenable in your attitude to your boss, more discreet in how you speak to him. After all, he has the power, has he not, to literally throw you on to the streets, if he chose to do so.'

'Don't be so bloody-minded, *kjære bror*. It wouldn't do any harm if you were a little more pleasant to my best friend.' To Noelle, 'You may not believe it, but he can charm the sun from behind the clouds if he wants to.'

'No,' said Noelle, still burning from her employer's reprimand, 'I wouldn't believe it.'

Kirsten threw back her head and laughed again. 'This is something new for you, Per. A woman who, instead of running after you, turns and runs the other way! Doesn't she intrigue you, doesn't she challenge you?'

'If she *challenges* me much more,' Per Arneson rasped, 'she will find herself without a job.' And he walked into his bedroom, slamming the door.

Ten minutes later he emerged, his fair hair still damp from the shower, having changed into casual clothes. His shirt, which was partly unbuttoned, was white and translucent, showing clearly the outline of his tanned body above the waist, the breadth of his chest, the fair hairs still glistening with undried water. His trousers were cream-coloured and hip-hugging, revealing the sensual movement of muscle as he walked lazily across the room.

Oh, God, Noelle thought, the man attracts me. No wonder the women come running. From head to toe he's like a magnet, a Pied Piper with the women scurrying behind, doing their damnedest to catch him.

As he poured himself a drink, she could not tear her eyes away, despising the feelings he could arouse in her merely by being within her sight. As he raised the glass to his lips, he caught her scrutiny and an eyebrow lifted. Did he know what he was doing to her? Of course he did, she thought furiously. Wasn't she reacting like all the other females of whom he talked with such scorn?

'We've helped ourselves to your private store,' Kirsten said, absent-mindedly, her thoughts on her work. 'I've had a drink. So has our guest.' She emphasized the final word.

Her brother caught the emphasis. 'Guest? Yours, not mine.'

Noelle, who was kneeling beside Kirsten, with the pattern spread out in front of them, straightened her back without rising, and felt in her trouser pocket. 'All right, I'll *pay* for the drink, Herr Arneson.'

'Keep your money, Miss Roberts,' he said coolly. 'I have plenty of it. I don't need yours. I'm supposed to be giving some of it to you, am I not, in the form of a regular weekly wage?'

'Kirsten,' said Noelle, still furious, 'how much would that drink have cost at the bar?'

'Oh, calm down,' Kirsten said. 'Don't let my big brother needle you.'

'But I'm just an employee,' Noelle persisted, in the face of her better judgment. 'Why should I be singled out from all the others for his charity?'

'All right, Miss Roberts,' Per Arneson rasped, 'pay for your drink.' He named a sum which filled Noelle with dismay. It seemed to contain so many *kroner*. 'You have to pay,' he said, with a taunting smile, plainly enjoying her discomfiture, 'for first class service, first class surroundings. First class company,' he added, his eyes glinting. 'After all, the owner's sister waited on you.'

He had called her bluff. Noelle reached into her pocket and drew out her purse. She emptied out the contents on to the white carpet and counted out the sum he had named. All the time she was counting – she was not yet fully accustomed to Norwegian currency – she was conscious of Per Arneson's sardonic eyes on her, eyes which she dared not meet, because she could not show this man that he had won.

When she had selected the necessary amount, there was little left to put back into the purse. He had not quite cleaned her out of money, but near enough to force her to ask Kirsten to help her out until she received her first pay cheque.

Noelle stood and went towards him, eyes full of rebellion, and placed the coins in his palm. He closed his fingers on them – and trapped her fingers, too. The unexpected action made her pulses race. She saw the exultant look in his eyes. Did he, she thought, have to enjoy his victory quite so blatantly?

'Per,' said Kirsten, watching them, 'you're not taking the money?'

In answer, he released Noelle's hand and slipped the coins into his pocket. 'The traditional way,' he mocked, 'for a rich man to get richer – at the expense of the poor. Is that not so, Miss Roberts?'

Noelle answered angrily, 'I would agree that most rich men are rich because they are unscrupulous and at some time in their lives have walked over those who have got in their way.'

'And I am unscrupulous?'

Noelle looked at the hard eyes and saw the raised eyebrows waiting for an answer. 'Totally,' she replied, 'in every aspect of your life. You would–' Discretion, signalling warnings, stopped her.

'Go on,' said her listener.

She could not resist such encouragement. Throwing discretion out of the glass doors which stood open to the view, she said, 'You would take advantage of every situation, every – every woman that came your way, if it were in your interest to do so.'

The level of anger to which she had aroused him was evident in every taut muscle in his body. He took a step towards her, but what he would have done had he not been interrupted by his sister, Noelle would never know.

'Oh, I like to hear you two together,' Kirsten said. 'It does me good to hear a woman stand up to my dear brother Per! I must write and tell our mother and father. Now return to your contemplation with me, Noelle, of this fabulous pattern I have dreamed up. Forget my brother, remember I'm your friend.'

Forget Per Arneson? Kirsten did not realize that she was asking the impossible.

CHAPTER THREE

EVERY evening, dinner was served in the traditional way. The waitresses, under the supervision of the *hovmester*, were each allocated four tables. From seven o'clock onwards people drifted in for their meal, and Noelle found her first evening waiting at table the most testing time of all.

To her surprise, at one of her tables she found that the assistant *direktör*, Roy Vikör, and his wife and child were taking their places. They were joined by the chief receptionist.

But when Noelle saw the *direktör* himself pushing through the swing doors and making his way to another of her tables – it bore a 'reserved' card – she almost turned and made for the kitchens. Was she, an inexperienced newcomer, supposed to serve the most important people in the hierarchy of the hotel?

It's not fair, she fumed, waiting with apparent meekness for the owner to seat himself comfortably at the table. She was in a quandary. Whom should she serve – the people who arrived first, or the owner, because he was the most important? She looked round agitatedly, but the head waiter was busy over the other side of the dining-room. The decision would have to be her own.

Holding her pad and pencil, she approached the owner's table. As she stood beside him and said, in a voice which could hardly be heard, 'Your order, please?' he looked up with some surprise.

'Are there not others you should be serving first? After all, I've just come.'

'I'm sorry. I thought that as you were the owner—'

'In these circumstances, my guests are more important than I am.' He looked up at her with a smile, but the smile was edged, like a wall topped with broken glass.

He motioned with his hand. 'Guests, then my colleagues, then me, in that order. However,' again that smile, 'you may find you're clever enough to cope with four tables at once. Most other waitresses do. Why not try?'

She swung away angrily and made for the guests' tables. There was a party of six, and as they selected dishes, changed their minds, chose other dishes, only to discard these, she grew confused and hot, knowing all the time that the sardonic eyes of Per Arneson were on her, watching, listening, and no doubt condemning her for her lack of guidance to her customers in helping them come to their final decisions.

With a stab of fear she thought, if I'm like this now, what will I do when I'm actually serving the food? What terrible mistakes will I make then?

At last everyone at the table had made up their minds and Noelle hurried into the kitchens to give the orders. Then she returned to take the order of the other guests. Since there were only two at that particular table, it did not take long.

On her way to serve the assistant *direktör* and his family, Noelle gave a quick, apprehensive glance at the owner. He was watching her with cold eyes and saw her hesitation. With an impatient gesture, he indicated the other table.

Roy Vikör, Per Arneson's deputy, looked up at her sympathetically. He spoke in English and was almost as fluent in the language as his employer. 'You are new? It is your first day? Cheer up,' he smiled, and his was genuine, unlike his employer's, 'you're not doing so badly. Dinner is always the worst. There is so much to remember and so much running about.' Noelle smiled with sheer relief. At last, someone who understood! 'If you smile like that at our guests, Fröken Roberts, they will forgive you anything, short of tipping the food into their laps!'

Noelle laughed and felt herself relax. Precisely and quickly, Roy Vikör gave the order for the entire table.

'Now go to Herr Arneson,' he directed. 'Don't look so afraid. He will not be angry with you for keeping him waiting, since it is your first day.'

But, Noelle thought, walking across to the last of the four tables, Herr Arneson doesn't like me, so Herr Arneson will take every opportunity to make me feel small and inefficient.

Per flicked a glance at her flushed face and looked back at the menu. In clear, terse tones he gave his order, adding, 'I would like some wine, please.'

She forgot the instructions of the head waiter and stood waiting dutifully for Per Arneson's wine order. He looked up at her, impatient again. 'You don't take orders for wine. Ask the wine waiter to bring the card.'

His voice was so sharp, Noelle felt the resentment welling up in her again. Why couldn't he be as understanding as his deputy? She replied, with defiant obedience, 'Yes, Herr Arneson, at once, Herr Arneson,' and almost winced at the look of fury he threw at her.

She realized she had gone too far and apologized. If she met him again that evening, she knew she would have to bear the brunt of his displeasure, expressed as cuttingly as only he knew how.

But she did not see him – or Kirsten – again that evening. Instead, she spent her spare time watching television – many of the films shown were English or American with Norwegian subtitles – and talking to Mark Anderson who, it seemed, in his shy way, was trying to get her to accept him as her 'special' boy-friend.

Noelle was in bed again that night before Maria and Sophia returned, and again they were accompanied by their boy-friends. This time they burst in and turned on the light, openly annoyed with her for being there, let alone in bed, although it was nearly one o'clock. The young men came into the room and peered at Noelle, smiling in such a way that she hunched herself on to her side away from them.

They laughed loudly and began making mild love to the

two girls, but Maria spoke in halting Norwegian, interspersed with Italian. By her tone of voice, it seemed she was sending them away. Reluctantly, the young men said good night, repeating in English, 'Good night, miss . . .'

When the men had gone, the two girls took their time in preparing for bed. It was obvious they did not care that they were keeping Noelle awake. They openly resented her conventional, sensible behaviour. Noelle wondered how long she could go on living this way, working so hard during the day that all she wanted to do in the evening was go to bed, yet when she got there, not being allowed to sleep.

The prospect – of making a mistake through tiredness, of being slow, of being accused by someone in authority of failing to rise to the necessary standards – frightened her.

Next morning it was an effort to drag herself from bed. The other girls had left by the time she was ready to go across to the hotel. It was late when she arrived and she had time for only a few pieces of crispbread and a hurried cup of coffee.

It was when breakfasts were over and she was on her way to the staff house for the morning coffee break that she met Per Arneson in the hotel foyer. He was studying the register at the reception desk and glanced up as she passed.

He looked at her keenly, watched her dragging footsteps for a moment and called, 'Miss Roberts, come over here, please.'

Slowly, obediently, she complied. She had no fight in her and she knew it showed. He motioned her into the small office at the rear of the reception area and closed the door.

'Is there something wrong? Do you not feel well?'

'There's nothing wrong with me, Herr Arneson.'

'But I can see there is, Miss Roberts. And it doesn't take a doctor to diagnose extreme tiredness. Is the job proving too much for you?'

She sighed. 'You would like me to say yes to that, wouldn't you? It would be such a good excuse for getting rid of someone as unsuitable as I am.'

'Miss Roberts, I'm trying to be understanding, I'm trying to be patient. Don't try that patience too far.'

'May I—' She looked round. 'May I sit down?' He motioned her to a chair. 'I don't think it's the job, although I must admit that anyone would need time to adjust to the strain of being on one's feet for such long periods. It's—' Could she tell him? She saw the question in his eyes and knew she would have to. 'It's having to share a room with Maria and Sophia.'

'I'm sorry,' he remarked acidly, 'that we can't provide you with the comfort and attention we lavish on our guests.'

He eyed her coldly and she took a breath to explain, but realized that if she did, it would amount to telling tales about her colleagues. So all she said was, 'I know nothing can be done about it. I'll just have to adjust.' At the door she said, 'Thank you for listening, Herr Arneson. And for your – sympathy.'

Sympathy? she thought ruefully as she went out. He had offered her none. He didn't even know the meaning of the word.

Again that evening, Per Arneson dined in the hotel dining-room. According to the head waiter, it was his custom to do so. That way, he said, the boss could keep an eye on both the staff and the welfare of his guests.

He dined always at the same table – Noelle's table. Would she, she wondered with dismay, have to wait on him for the entire length of her service on his staff?

To Noelle's delight, Kirsten dined with her brother. She had not seen Kirsten all day. When she had been free, Kirsten had been out. As Noelle stood waiting for Per Arneson's order, Kirsten squeezed her hand.

'Don't look so unhappy. You're doing fine. Per, Noelle's doing fine, isn't she?'

Without looking up from his contemplation of the menu, Per said, 'If Miss Roberts requires a reference as to her character and performance as a member of my staff, she should apply to the assistant *direktör*, not to me.'

Noelle flushed at the entirely uncalled-for humiliation he had subjected her to, using his sister's good-natured encouragement to that end.

'If I needed a reference, Herr Arneson, I certainly wouldn't—'

His head came up and his eyes released a warning shot across her face. It brought stinging colour to her cheeks and a halting apology to her lips.

Kirsten said, 'She was right to retaliate, Per. Why are you always trying to put Noelle in her place?'

With infinite care, he stood the menu on the table, then he sat back and fixed his eyes on Noelle, although addressing his sister. 'First, she was not right to retaliate. One cannot "retaliate" against a simple statement of fact, which is what it was. Also, there is an unpalatable but vital truth she will have to learn if she is to continue on the staff of this hotel for the full three months – namely, that she does not argue with the boss. Second,' now his eyes grew sardonic, 'I haven't yet decided just where Miss Roberts' "place" is. Being a man, I can use my imagination . . .' He watched with amusement the anger which flared behind her eyes, then he gave the order.

As Per and Kirsten were leaving the dining-room, having finished their meal, Kirsten caught Noelle as she hurried past. 'Are you free this evening after this lot,' she indicated the diners, 'have gone?' Yes, Noelle told her. 'Dress up a bit,' Kirsten said, 'and join me in the bar. Don't take fright as you usually do. It's time you came out of your shell,' she appealed to her brother again, 'isn't it, Per?' He had no answer to give.

'In the bar?' Noelle echoed. 'But—'

'There's no need to look so *hunted*!' Kirsten joked. 'We Norwegians don't eat our visitors alive. We're a kindly, highly civilized people.'

Noelle laughed. 'I've discovered that for myself in the short time I've been here.'

Per looked at her with interest. 'You feel at home in Norway, Miss Roberts? You must come here again some time – for a holiday, without the work attached to it.'

'As our guest, Per,' Kirsten asked eagerly, 'instead of an employee?'

'As our *guest*, of course,' adding, with a brief, mocking smile, 'provided she books through the usual channels and has sufficient money to cover her stay.'

'Per!' his sister reprimanded. 'You're at it again, putting Noelle in her place.'

His eyes darkened. 'One day I will,' he muttered. 'And that, Miss Roberts, is a promise, not a threat!'

The bar occupied a corner of the hotel lounge. It was constructed of pine, with pine panelling and high stools to match.

Noelle, after a brief glance round, found Kirsten. She was, for once, hemmed in on only one side by young men. On her other was an empty stool which it seemed she had been saving for Noelle. On the other side of the empty stool sat the owner of the hotel.

He was relaxed. In his hand was a glass which was resting on the bar top. He wore a navy open-necked shirt and matching trousers, the dark colour a dramatic contrast to the glinting fairness of his hair. And he was as big an obstacle to Noelle's occupation of the empty stool as if a wall of fire burned and crackled in the intervening space.

Kirsten had not seen her, so Noelle made her way warily towards the group of young men who crowded round her friend. If she could attach herself to the side of them, like a bubble joining a patch of foam, staying there unnoticed until Per Arneson went away ...

But it was plain Per Arneson had no thought of going away. He half-swung round on his stool and fixed her with his eyes. If she walked away now, she had the ridiculous feeling that he would rap out an order across the room, telling her to occupy the seat beside him or else she would suffer a cut in salary.

Not wishing to be the focal point of interest for all the other occupants of the lounge, Noelle took a grip on herself and with slow, reluctant footsteps made her way towards him.

As she drew near, he swung to face the bar again, apparently satisfied that his unspoken order had been obeyed. When she put a foot on the rail and hoisted herself on to the stool, he gave an ironic smile and lifted his glass in a silent, mocking toast.

Kirsten became aware of her then and flung a welcoming arm round her neck. 'You made it! And you've put on something nice. That's good. Per,' she bent forward to address her brother, 'isn't Noelle great when she's dressed up?'

Turning his head, Per looked her over, his eyes dwelling on the white close-fitting top with lacing at the neckline, but which Noelle had left partially unlaced and below it the ankle-length floral skirt. His eyes lifted to study the long, soft brown hair framing the attractive, but at that moment defiant, profile. That the profile only partly satisfied him and that he wanted the opportunity to study the whole of her face in order to complete his investigations and deliver his verdict, was obvious by the way he said her name.

'Noelle?'

Her heart jerked crazily, her head swung round, making her hair swirl in a cloud round her shoulders. Her lips parted with astonishment – and something else. Was it fear? Her name had sounded so sweet on his lips that she wanted to hear him say it again and again . . .

The eyes that looked into her eyes were no longer icy. They were quizzical, enigmatic and heart-stopping. 'Now,' he said, propping an elbow on the bar and supporting his chin in his hand, 'if I were to agree with my sister that you look "great" when you're dressed up, it would imply, would it not, that you don't look great when you're not dressed up. For which you would never forgive me. Is that right,

Noelle?'

Under that half amused, half provocative gaze, Noelle found her colour rising again, which the man beside her watched with a reflective smile.

'Don't bother to answer your sister's question, Herr Arneson. Even if you paid me a compliment, it would only be to satisfy your sister. And in any case, I wouldn't believe it.'

He was not annoyed as she had guessed he might be. 'Then,' he said blandly, 'the way is clear for me to pay you that compliment, since I'm safe in the knowledge that you will not believe it. Yes, Kirsten, your friend does indeed look – great.' He straightened from speaking to his sister. 'A drink, Noelle?'

Did he have to keep speaking her name in that soft, seductive way? She opened her purse and looked at the few coins inside it. She certainly could not waste them on a drink. 'No, thank you, Herr Arneson.'

'You can't occupy a seat at the bar and not have a drink.'

Did he have to persist? She shook her head. 'I haven't enough – I mean, I don't want—' Involuntarily she clutched her purse.

'Are you short of cash?' The question was sharp, catching her unawares.

'Well, I – until I'm—' How could she lower herself to tell this man that until he paid her salary at the end of the week, she would have no spare money for luxuries, only for necessities?

But he was quick, too quick, to understand. 'Until you're paid? I shall instruct Roy Vikör, my deputy, to give you an advance on your pay.' Noelle shook her head, but he was not even looking at her. 'Now, a drink.' He glanced round the lounge. 'When Sonja is free, I shall order one for you. Kirsten?' His sister turned from the young man to whom she was speaking. 'Where's Sonja?'

Kirsten shrugged. 'You should know, Per. She's your current woman.'

Per's eyes hardened, intending to crush, but he did not deny the assertion.

'Per, *kjæreste*!' A woman approached from a group of people in a darkened corner. Noelle, with a curiously cold feeling, guessed that the word that had followed his name was an endearment.

The woman, instead of taking her place behind the bar, rested a hand on Per's arm and gazed up at him. Per did not respond as the girl had obviously hoped he would. As Noelle watched, she wondered that any man could resist those enticing hazel eyes, the silky fair hair, the tip-tilted nose.

'*I aften*?' Sonja whispered coaxingly.

'No,' curtly, 'not this evening. Will you get a drink for—' He motioned towards Noelle. 'For Miss Roberts. A Martini?' Noelle shook her head, but again he did not appear to see. 'And the same again for me.' To Noelle, 'I'm in your debt.' At her frown he added, 'That drink in my apartment.'

'Oh, but I—'

'In your apartment, *elskling*?' Sonja pouted and looked venomously at Noelle. 'You have thrown me over for another woman?'

Per slanted a sardonic glance at Noelle. 'Not yet, Sonja, not yet. The lady is not willing.' Now his smile grew mocking. 'Is she, Noelle?'

Sonja sighed. 'Ah, but that is good news. Now I will get your drinks.'

As they waited, Per asked, 'Have you seen much of our countryside yet, Noelle?'

Noelle shook her head. 'On my first day off, I'm hoping to go for a boat trip along the fjords. Kirsten says the ferries run regularly.'

Sonja brought the drinks and Per handed over the money. He said, as Sonja served another customer, 'There are some good outings laid on for tourists. You must try one or two while you're here. Get Kirsten to take you. Or, better still,' the smile he gave was not sincere, 'your tame boy-friend from the kitchens.'

'Mark Anderson? He's not my boy-friend.'

'No? Then why is he hovering over there in the background watching us like the proverbial hawk? Does he think I'm going to make off with you like a wolf into the mountains?'

In spite of herself, Noelle laughed at the picture the words conjured up. 'I don't think you could ever be so – so hard up for feminine company that you would be reduced to wanting mine, Herr Arneson.'

'No?' He caught her chin, forcing her face round. 'You think a man would have to be "reduced" to wanting you as a companion?' He netted her eyes and she could not tear them away. The touch of his fingers on her face was enough in itself to set her heart racing, without the softness of his words or the probing, disarming gaze. 'You underrate yourself, Miss Roberts, you sadly underrate your attractions.'

Noelle jerked herself free of his touch. 'What are you doing,' she threw at him, 'trying out your technique to discover whether it works with me as it apparently does on all the other women you have known? Or,' lowering her voice, 'making your girl-friend jealous?' Noelle indicated Sonja who was watching every movement Per made, every response Noelle gave to his words and actions. Her eyes were vicious with resentment and reproach.

'Is it working, Per?' came the dry question from his sister. 'That magical charm – has it still the same appeal?'

A few moments passed while Per studied the averted face of the girl beside him. 'Evidently not,' he replied. 'You have a peculiar friend, Kirsten. It seems she prefers me when I'm being unpleasant to her. When I try to be agreeable and friendly, she snaps and sinks her teeth into me.'

Kirsten leaned forward and spoke across Noelle. 'You'll be paying me that money yet, Per.'

'Noelle?' He spoke her name so abruptly she turned her head and once again found her eyes caught by his. It was no use, she could not tear them away. He smiled and it was a satisfied smile. 'I think not,' he murmured. 'There's time, plenty of time.'

'Noelle?' Now the voice came from behind her. Mark Anderson had found the courage to approach her. 'I'm off for a walk. Coming?'

'Oh, don't go, Noelle,' Kirsten said, smiling. 'You're depriving my brother of his favourite pastime – playing cat and mouse with a woman. You're giving him such a good run for his money. He usually makes a killing at the first meeting.'

Noelle looked at Per, taking no pains to hide her anger. 'Tell your brother, Kirsten, that he's wasting his time. I'd much prefer it if he would stick strictly to the employer-employee relationship.' She slipped down from her stool.

Kirsten burst out laughing. 'That puts you where you belong, Per – out in the cold. Where are you going, Noelle? For a walk with your boy-friend?'

Mark Anderson coloured to be so described, but with a touch of defiance, Noelle nodded. As they walked away from the bar, Noelle heard Sonja say huskily,

'Now that girl has gone, you can give all your attention to me, *elskling* . . .'

For some time after their walk, Noelle chatted to Mark in the staff lounge. Then, with a touch of apology, she told him she was tired. He looked a little bleak as she left him, but he made no move to delay her. Noelle wondered how he had ever found the courage to approach her in the first place.

It was not long before she had showered in one of the bathrooms and was ready for bed. When the door burst open and the room was flooded with light, she was awakened from the beginnings of a dream, a dream which from that moment started to turn into something of a nightmare.

Maria came in first, pulling her boy-friend behind her. Sophia followed with hers. On seeing Noelle, one of the young men started to leave, but Maria tugged him back.

'Don't mind her,' she said, and pulled the young man's head down to kiss him. Sophia did likewise, pushing her boy-friend down on to the bed. Someone turned out the light and two girls giggled in response to the young men's whisperings.

Noelle flung back the bed covers, reached for her torch, found her wrap and stumbled barefoot from the room. In the corridor she blinked under the harsh light. The daze of being awoken so suddenly had not left her. Where could she go? How long would her room companions keep her from bed? She had no idea of the time, but since the house was silent, she guessed it must be well past midnight.

The stair carpet was soft against her bare feet, and as she pushed open the door of the staff lounge and switched on the light, she held her breath. But the room was empty. The clock on the wall told her it was half past one. She sat in an armchair and waited. But, she told herself, that was no good. She would have to read. On a shelf there was a collection of paperback novels, some of them printed in English.

Drawing her feet under her, Noelle curled up in an armchair and opened the book she had chosen. She read a few pages and yawned. After three more pages, her head drooped and she had to jerk it upright. At the end of the chapter, her eyes closed and she drifted into a dream.

For the second time that night, a door bursting open had her shuddering to wakefulness. When she saw the man who was staring at her so unbelievingly, so – angrily, the book slipped unheeded from her lap. The sight of her employer striding towards her had her petrified.

His words did not help to quell her fears. 'What the hell are you doing in here? Or,' with a sneer, 'is it a practice of yours to get yourself into your nightclothes, sit in a public room and wait for the highest bidder?'

The colour burned her cheeks as she unwound from the chair and faced him, pulling her wrap around her. She felt for the belt, but it was missing. It must have fallen off in the bedroom. She opened her mouth – but she could think of nothing to say. How could she explain her extraordinary presence in the staff lounge at that time of the morning?

With a nervous gesture she pushed her hair from her face, then wished she hadn't, because he stared at her features so intently.

'Well,' he said at last, 'what are you waiting for? For me to name a price?'

Again she coloured, and this time his humiliating words stung her to retaliate. 'Only you of all my acquaintances would speak to me like that – probably because it annoys you that I refuse to come when you beckon. You would like me to answer "yes" to your question, wouldn't you, then you could play around with me as you do with all your women friends.' Unexpectedly, fatigue overcame her and she sank on to a chair. 'At least,' she muttered, 'it would give me a bed for the night.'

His eyes half closed. 'If I were convinced you really knew what you were saying ...' There was a long pause, then, 'What's the matter with your own bed?'

She did not answer – how could she, without giving away Maria and Sophia?

'Let me guess,' he went on. 'You found yourself – how shall I put it? – one too many? And our narrow-minded Miss Roberts—'

'I am *not* narrow-minded,' she cried. 'How would you like it if – if—' She eyed the door. 'I'm – I'm not staying here with you. I'm going out—' But before she had reached the other side of the room, Per had the door closed and his back to it.

'Your feet are bare. And besides,' he looked her over estimatingly, 'in that alluring outfit,' the wrap had fallen open again, revealing her clinging nightdress, 'you're dressed more for – er – indoor activities, rather than outdoor.' His eyes reached her face. 'No, on second thoughts, you look too tired even for that. Before you collapse on your feet, tell me what has happened.' Still she was silent. He smiled sardonically. 'Go ahead. I'm broad-minded. I wouldn't fire your room-mates – or anyone – from their jobs because of their morals – or lack of them.'

So, haltingly, Noelle explained how she came to be asleep in the staff lounge in the early hours.

'How long has this been going on?' Per asked.

'Since I came.'

'No wonder you looked so tired when I questioned you yesterday morning. Why didn't you tell me then?'

She did not reply and he was silent for some time. Then he said, 'There's only one thing to do. Come with me.' He held the door open, then caught her wrist as she passed in front of him. She tried to twist it from his grasp, but he held fast, smiling and saying, 'Just a precaution. If I let you go, you might carry out your threat to run away.' He looked down the length of her. 'And it pains me to think of those slim, tender feet getting torn by the grit and stones outside. Especially,' his smile was taunting, 'as I'm paying you so much to be on them most of the day.'

He stopped in front of a door and with his free hand, felt for some keys. He selected one and opened the door, pulling her behind him into a room. It was a bedroom.

'Mine,' he said. 'I use it when my parents come to stay and take possession of my room in my apartment. Tonight, and for an unknown number of nights, this room is yours.' His eyes mocked her. 'Whether or not I occupy it at the same time as yourself is entirely up to you.'

Noelle stared round. 'Why are you allowing me to come in here?'

'Why?' He shrugged. 'Because I don't want a member of my staff to be all the time,' he paused '*trett* – weary, tired. What else do you want me to say – because you are a friend of my sister's, therefore I give you preferential treatment?'

Again the desire to retaliate surged through her, but the kindness of his gesture – and it was kind, however unkindly he was offering it – in allowing her the use of his room prevented her indignation from breaking through.

The room was of a generous size compared with the one she and the two other girls had been sharing. The wood of the furniture was pine – the bed-head, the built-in wardrobes, the dressing-table. The carpet was green, as were the curtains and bedspread. There was taste here, and elegance and comfort – too much, far too much for a girl who was merely a pawn in Per Arneson's very large and profitable game of chess, a girl who in a strictly temporary capacity was working for him in just one of his many hotels.

Per looked at his watch. 'Two o'clock. Isn't it time all good little girls – and bad ones, also,' with a smile, 'were in bed?'

She caught at the edges of the wrap which would keep falling open, then hesitated. If she took it off in front of this man, would he construe what he saw beneath it as an invitation?

He motioned towards the bed. 'Try it for size. It's a double one. You're so slim you might get lost in it. Then what would my sister say? I cannot run the risk of losing her best friend!'

Noelle looked at him uncertainly, refusing to give smile for smile. But could she really expect this man to turn his back while she – partially – disrobed? The wrap fell away from her shoulders and she flung it on a chair. She looked at him anxiously, trying to guess his reaction. Of course he was looking at her, looking his fill, enjoying – there was no doubt about it – the sight of her slender curves outlined beneath the thin material of her nightdress.

She turned back the covers and got into bed, sliding down into their smooth, soothing warmth. Her head pressed into the pillow as she gazed up at him. Her hair spread over it, and the expression in her fatigue-large eyes was a mixture of exhaustion, pleasure and contentment.

'Thank you, Herr Arneson,' she whispered.

With a half-smile, he looked down at her. 'While you're in my bed, we cannot have such formality! Call me Per.'

'Thank you – Per,' she murmured.

'Yes, that sounds right.' His smile warmed her through, bringing a glow to her face. Here was the Arneson charm which he kept strictly for the women he wished to coax into his private, secret world. Looking up into his fine-featured face, in which arrogance and ruthlessness walked hand in hand, Noelle had to acknowledge that it would be dangerously easy to succumb to that charm. At that particular moment, if he had followed up the advantage he undoubtedly had over her, the resistance she knew her self-respect would demand – the idea of being just another of his collection of women was abhorrent to her – would be very difficult to stir into any sort of meaningful life.

She closed her eyes because it was essential that he must not read the treacherous thoughts that were invading her mind.

He went to the door and said from a distance, 'In the morning, you will move your belongings into here. In there is a bath and shower.' He motioned to a room which led off the bedroom. 'The door is locked. In fairness to the others, it will have to remain locked.' He smiled tauntingly. 'Allowing you to occupy my bed is one thing, allowing you to share my bath and shower is quite another.'

With this he left her, and she was asleep almost as soon as the door was closed.

'So,' said Kirsten impishly, when she and Noelle were sitting over afternoon tea in Per's flat, 'my brother has put you in your place again – his bed!'

Noelle laughed. 'If you put it that way, it sounds terrible.'

Kirsten shrugged. 'Why terrible? Most girls would be delighted to be in Per's bed.' She smiled. 'Not alone, of course, like you. Anyway, what's wrong with my brother? He has plenty to offer, money, position—'

Noelle broke in, horrified at having offended her friend, 'There's nothing wrong with your brother . . .'

Kirsten burst out laughing. 'I must tell him that. "My

dear friend Noelle says there is nothing wrong with you".' Before Noelle could remonstrate she said, 'Now let's plunge into that pool out there before there's a crush of people.' She rose, urging her friend to do the same.

But Noelle said, 'You go, Kirsten. I'll stay here and watch. I'm too lazy to go back to my—' she looked up, 'Per's room—'

'I like the sound of that,' said Kirsten, grinning.

Noelle went on, ignoring her friend's banter, 'To get my swimsuit.'

'Borrow one of mine. It's sure to fit.' Kirsten disappeared into her bedroom. 'Here you are,' she called. 'Try it on. Our measurements are about the same.'

But Noelle discovered that not only was the swimsuit briefer than her own, it was tighter. Kirsten had not realized that she was smaller built than Noelle. When Noelle protested that she was not decent enough to go out in public in the two small blue pieces of material Kirsten called a swimsuit, Kirsten disagreed firmly.

'But if your brother sees me like this – after all, I'm really only his employee – he'll fire me.'

'If that's what you think, then you know very little about male psychology. He won't fire you, he'll promote you! Anyway, he's busy in his office, so forget him. Come on, who's first in?'

They had been swimming for some time before Noelle became aware of her employer's presence. She had been too distracted by the beauty all around her as she lay floating on her back. There was the intense blueness of the sky, the magnificent mountains, and below, the waters of the fjord, busy with boats and ferries moving backwards and forwards from the landing stage in the village, across the great stretch of water, to disappear round the corner into the next fjord.

Hotel guests joined them in the pool, shouting to each other and throwing beach balls. It was only when Kirsten lifted an arm and shouted, 'Hi, Per!' that Noelle saw him.

There was a strange and frightening twist inside her as she looked up at him looking down at her. It was then that she remembered the briefness of the swimsuit she had borrowed, and regretted her impulse in accepting Kirsten's offer to lend it to her.

And Per was so plainly enjoying her embarrassment. He stood, hands in pockets, the white shirt on again, but unbuttoned to the waist, revealing the fine hairs which covered his chest. They were darker than the hair on his head, Noelle noted abstractedly, then reproached her eyes for noticing such an intimate fact.

With a swift movement, his shirt was off and flung on to a folding chair, his trousers unzipped and thrown to join it. With his swimming briefs already in place, he was plunging in a curve into the water. He was up in a moment, pushing back his dripping hair with both hands. He had surfaced near to Noelle and gave her a brief derisive grin as his eyes raked her from top to toe, then he thrust himself forward through the water to the other end of the pool.

Now Per was there, Noelle could not relax sufficiently to enjoy herself, so, without a word to Kirsten, she swam towards the steps. She hoisted herself on to the bottom rung, but her ankle was gripped in a circle of iron, and she was pulled back shrieking into the water. Arms came round her and she struggled violently.

'No, no!' she shouted, gasping as the water threatened to close over her. Per was holding her down and laughing into her face, threatening at the same time to push her under.

'Submit,' he said, 'submit or I'll—'

'I'll submit!' she shrieked, and a hard, ruthless mouth covered hers. It was over so quickly no one could possibly have noticed, but Per did not release her at once. Instead he gazed into her indignant face, his eyes gleaming, his damp face broadened into a mocking smile.

'That's right, Per,' Kirsten gasped, pulling alongside them, 'play your little game with your usual expertise and you can't fail to win.'

'You be quiet,' he said, jerking his head dismissively, 'don't you know when your company is unwanted?'

Kirsten lifted her hand in an ironic salute and swam away.

'Please let me go, Herr—'.

'Say Per.'

'Per. What will the other members of staff think?'

'They're thinking it already. They've already put us into bed together. It hasn't taken long for the fact that you are sleeping in my private room to get around on the hotel grapevine.'

Noelle struggled to free herself. Indignation, coupled with the slipperiness of her body, gave her the advantage and she got away from him. She made frantically for the steps and this time managed to scramble up them unmolested – only to come face to face with Sonja.

'You,' said Sonja, 'leave Per Arneson alone. He is not yours. He's mine.'

Per appeared beside them, dripping, smiling, hands on hips, his chest expanding and contracting as his lungs filled with air.

'*Kjæreste*,' Sonja appealed to him, 'is it not true? You are mine.' She hung on to his arm, wet though it was, and gazed into his face.

With firmness he removed her arm from his. '*Nei*. It is not true.'

Sonja said sulkily, 'Have it your way. But I am yours, that you cannot deny.' Her dark eyes rested on Noelle, conveying an unmistakable warning.

Kirsten hoisted herself out of the pool and came towards them, the water running off her. 'Just look at my brother,' she said, 'basking in the adoration of two women.'

'Leave me out of it,' muttered Noelle, looking defiantly at Per. 'I adore no man. I never have. I never will.'

'Dangerous words, Miss Roberts. You may live to eat them yet, as your countrymen say.'

Noelle did not rise to Per's challenge. Instead she turned

to her friend. 'I'm going in, Kirsten. Is there a towel?'

'Plenty. I'll show you.'

In Kirsten's room, towelling herself, Noelle asked, 'Who is Sonja? She's surely not just an employee of Per's? She seems too – well, superior for that.'

Kirsten said, with interest, 'So you've noticed something different about her? She comes from a wealthy Oslo family. She's a linguist like Per, and can speak a number of languages, almost as many as he can. Also she handles foreign currency like an expert, which is one reason why she helps behind the bar. She can converse with people of the many different nationalities who stay here. Our parents live in Oslo,' Kirsten added. 'They visit Per at a number of his hotels. When they come here they have his room – it's larger than mine – and Per sleeps across at the staff house.'

'So he told me last night.'

'Yes, last night.' Kirsten looked at Noelle reflectively. 'Per told me he actually returned here after seeing you into his bed.' She shook her head. 'I don't think any other woman would have done that to him.'

Noelle frowned. 'Done what?'

'Sent him away.'

Noelle laughed uncomfortably. 'I'm different.'

Kirsten laughed, too, rubbing her hands expectantly. 'I'm beginning to think you are. I, for one, am enjoying the tussle between you. And I'm still not sure who is going to win.'

CHAPTER FOUR

A FEW days later in Per's apartment, Kirsten was working on the dress she was making while Noelle idly made sketches of ankle-length dresses on a large sheet of paper Kirsten had given her.

The phone rang and Kirsten answered. It was, she said, an old boy-friend of hers who had arrived in the village for a few hours to see her. She tidied her hair, pressed some lip-stick over her lips and was gone almost before Noelle had realized it. Kirsten called, 'Stay there, don't go away just because I've gone out. Carry on with your doodlings and sketches.'

But Noelle did not particularly care for the idea of being there when the owner of the hotel returned. He often took time off in the afternoon and would, quite naturally, take the opportunity of relaxing in the comfort of his apartment.

Although Noelle started to gather up her work almost as soon as her friend had gone, she had left it too late. The door opened and her employer walked in. He did not seem surprised to find her there alone. Noelle supposed that he had met his sister on her way out.

Flustered by his unexpected appearance, Noelle said, 'I'm sorry, Herr Arneson. I'm just going.'

'Why?'

As she scrabbled about on the floor, picking up pencils and scraps of paper, he came to stand over her. At his question, she looked up and up, the whole length of his body to his face. The sudden intimacy of his nearness had her heart drumming. He was wearing a formal suit, the trousers cut to fit the strong muscularity of his legs, the jacket sitting well on the intimidating breadth of his shoulders. From that angle he assumed the proportions of a giant and seemed almost as threatening. She remembered with a sensation of intense pleasure the kiss he had given her a few days before in the swimming pool, and the sweet remembrance made his proximity even more disturbing.

She straightened to face him, her cheeks warm with the excitement of his closeness. He was smiling his tantalizing half-smile, something that was between a taunt and a lure. A certain look, the slightest hint of capitulation on her part would, she was convinced, bring his arms about her and his lips possessively on hers. She sensed that that was what he was waiting for. No doubt, she thought bitterly, with most other women he did not have to wait so long.

'Why?' she answered his question. 'Because this is your apartment and you don't want me here. Kirsten has gone out, so—'

'Who said I don't want you here?'

Her look challenged him boldly. 'No one, Herr Arneson. I'm perfectly sure you do want me here, and for one purpose. But any woman would fulfil that purpose as far as you're concerned, wouldn't they? I'm sorry,' she made for the door, 'I don't play those games, so you see, from your point of view I'm a dead loss.'

'You would do well,' he eyed her narrowly, taking in her tight denim pants – she had washed them since her journey from England – and the black ribbed, high-necked top, 'to curtail your bluntness a little more. And a little more, shall we say, tact, towards your employer would be a good idea, too, sometimes.'

She coloured slightly, but not with embarrassment. This man was an expert at running his hand over her fur and making it stand on end. 'It's hardly fair, Herr Arneson, for you to play an interested, slightly lustful male at one moment, and the next turn back into the imperious, autocratic employer.'

He took a step towards her. 'You, Miss Roberts, will go too far one day. A lesson you have to learn is that frankness can be as damaging in certain situations as deviousness and dishonesty. If I were simply your employer and not also the brother of your friend, you would not presume to speak to me as you do. Be honest and admit it.'

In spite of the anger she felt towards him, in spite of the humiliation he could so cleverly make her feel, she apologized, her eyes to the ground. Then she went out, closing the door behind her.

He opened it and called after her, 'Where are you going?'

'I don't know. Somewhere, anywhere . . .'

She put her things in her room, pulled on a waist-length jacket and went down the stairs.

She had only seen the village in the evening when the shops had been shut. Now she wanted to get the feel of the place with life in it, instead of when it had been put to sleep for the night by the shopkeepers.

Per met her outside. It looked as though he had been about to come and find her. He had changed into casual clothes and wore a belted jacket. Strange, she thought, how he could shed the executive, slightly despotic air he wore while on duty, every part of him the affluent, efficient hotel owner, and get into the skin of a relaxed, indolent playboy.

Which he really was, and which he affected to be, Noelle did not know him well enough to decide. She eyed him with a touch of suspicion. Perhaps he was both. He was, after all, a self-confessed womanizer. Even his sister had admitted that. But wasn't he also the hard, ruthless businessman, with a chain of thriving hotels under his command?

That he could transfer that ruthlessness to his dealings with women Noelle had no doubt. If he wanted a woman out of his life, if he wanted to displace her with another – someone new and therefore more interesting, more intriguing – he would tear her out without qualm, without pity, like a finished month out of a calendar.

Now, as she made for the village, he matched his steps to hers. Her frankness put her feelings into her mouth. 'I'd rather go alone, thank you.'

He did not reprove her for her frankness this time. Instead, he gave her a one-sided smile. 'Forget me. Imagine I'm not here. I shall not say a word. I shall be your shadow.'

She had to smile back. It would be easier to forget a growling lion walking beside her than this man. When she stopped to gaze in the window of a souvenir shop, he stopped. When she went in to buy something – a paperknife bearing the name of the village, a few postcards – he went in, too. The shopkeeper knew him, of course, and they chatted for a few moments.

When Noelle stopped at another shop to look at a collection of white wool coats, gay with embroidery and 'troll' fasteners, he looked, first at the coats, then at her. When she ventured into the shop and felt the sweaters, thick and warm, neck-hugging and bright with woven colours, he followed. She picked one from a pile, tried it against her and put it down. She gazed at it, touched it again with her fingertips, sighed – and walked on. Eventually she left the shop empty-handed.

Outside he said, 'Why did you not buy that sweater? It looked your size.'

'Too expensive.'

With that provocative half-smile, 'Am I not paying you enough, then?'

She answered obliquely, 'I was aware before I came of what you would be paying me.'

He laughed. 'A tactful, if evasive, reply. But it is still obviously not sufficient to allow you to buy what you, being English, might term a "luxury", but which in the climate of my country is, in the coldness of winter, a necessity.'

'Since I won't be here in the winter, I needn't strain my financial resources to buy one, need I?'

He frowned for a moment, then said, 'But you have cold days in England, too. And,' with a smile, 'not only in winter.'

'Do you know England well, Herr Arneson?'

'Yes, very well. And the name is Per.'

'Herr Arneson.'

He smiled, without amusement, at her obstinacy, and his eyes glittered as if at a challenge. 'You cannot forget at this moment that I am your employer. Why don't you sometimes look upon me as your friend's brother?'

'Because when I do, *Herr Arneson,* you immediately assume an advantage over me and turn into my employer. So from now on, I'm taking no chances. I shall always regard you as my employer.'

His eyes were glittering again. 'I have it in my power, *Miss Roberts,* to create a situation in which you would have to regard me as – something very different from an employer.'

She coloured slightly. 'I'm sure you have, Herr Arneson, and I'm also sure that, if it were to your advantage and you would benefit materially,' she took a breath, 'physically from such a situation, you would not hesitate to create it.'

They were climbing now and he strode a few steps ahead, placing himself in front of her. His hands were in his pockets, but he looked perfectly capable of placing them round her neck. 'Are you challenging me, Miss Roberts?'

Her eyes opened exaggeratedly wide. 'Of *course* not, Herr Arneson.'

He seemed to check his breath as he gazed, with something approaching anger, into her face. Then he relaxed and they continued their walk. Noelle congratulated herself on winning at least one point against him. But something inside her trembled a little at the thought that he would not forget and at the first opportunity would go out of his way to get even with her.

One thing, she thought joyously, she had proved to herself – and she hoped, to him – that she was not one of those women to whom he had referred when she had first met him who 'ran towards him, arms outstretched'.

In an effort to lift the conversation to a less personal note,

Noelle asked, 'Do you often visit England?'

'I have numerous business interests there, so I'm in your country at fairly regular intervals.' He smiled quickly at her. 'I almost regard it as my second home.'

'Because you have a sister who's been studying there?'

He shrugged. 'I happen to like the place. And the people. Especially,' again with that swift smile, 'the women.'

Noelle stopped abruptly. It was, she told herself, to look at the view, but knew that she was not being entirely honest. This man and his women! She ought to hate him, but, and it dismayed her to have to admit it, she could not hate a man who attracted her to strongly, whose charm lay in wait beneath the surface of his personality like a dangerous lure, like an invisible snare, like a man-trap – no, a woman-trap, hidden in the undergrowth.

She gave herself to the view. It was magnificent. They were high up the hill now, and overlooking the village which was sheltered on three sides by great mountains. The fourth side, where the fjord rippled and shone in the sunlight, was like an open doorway, stretching into the blue, hazy distance.

Per looked, too. He gestured. 'With those mountains, this village is a sun-trap. Hence the fruit trees as far as you can see. In the spring the pink and white blossom against the background of the mountains is something you wouldn't forget in a hurry if you saw it. In autumn, the apples ripen by the roadside. You could, if you wanted, reach up your hand and pick one. But no one does, because they are the property of the fruit farmers.' He looked at her. 'You're surprised. Why?'

'To see all these fruit trees. I've always regarded Norway as a cold country.'

'We're lucky. The Gulf Stream is kind to us. It carries warmth and sunshine right along our coastline. Although Norway is far north geographically, it's a warm country in the summer and the mildness of the climate in the spring astonishes our visitors.'

Noelle's eyes mirrored her surprise, then they roamed, drinking in the beauty, resting on the snow which lay on the mountain tops, moving down to look at the pine trees growing in abundance over the lower hills. Everywhere was green, kind to the eyes and to the mind. The road was little more than a track, but now and then a car would pass on its way to one of the houses – modern chalets most of them, many constructed largely of wood.

'It was badly damaged here during the war,' Per said seriously. 'Now it has been completely rebuilt. I think, of all the places in which I have hotels, I like this the most. When I come here I find a calmness invade me, a contentment, a peace.' He turned to her with a smile. 'Except when I meet a rebellious young woman who is constantly asserting her rights as an individual, and who will not subdue her tongue even when she is speaking to her employer.'

'There you are,' she said triumphantly. 'At the touch of a button you change from my equal to my superior, from my friend's brother to the man who pays my wages. Which is exactly what I was trying to tell you earlier.'

He laughed. 'I think, at this moment, we should forget everything but that we are a man and woman out for a walk together. Does the idea please you?'

Please her? The idea tormented her, the idea of being woman to this man. What would it be like, a treacherous voice inside her asked, to be this man's 'woman'? To mean more to him than any other member of the opposite sex? The thought attracted her powerfully, and she had to tussle with the feelings it aroused. But, she reproached herself, what right had she to think that she possessed any quality that would make him want to regard her as more precious than any other woman? He had, his sister said, an 'insatiable appetite for women'. That alone should make her hate him. But that was something she simply could not bring herself to do . . .

They strolled down the hill, passing the church and reaching the village. For a while they stood near the landing stage at which the ferry berthed. The ship was far away across the fjord, its trail feathering out behind it. It was moving towards them and a line of cars and a group of passengers awaited their turn to board the ferry when it arrived.

Per took Noelle's hand. 'I will buy you a cup of delicious Norwegian coffee. In the village there's a cafeteria adjoining a hotel, a rival of mine.'

He held her hand as they walked to the cafeteria, and although Noelle made an attempt to withdraw her fingers from his, she did not try very hard. Her arm came alive at his touch, and the feeling spread like a consuming fire through her body. At that moment, walking hand in hand with Kirsten's brother was all she could ever ask of life.

Per relinquished her hand as they entered the cafeteria and Noelle felt a deep thrust of disappointment. 'Find a seat,' he said, 'while I buy the coffee.'

Per, who seemed well acquainted with the woman behind the self-service counter, laughed and chatted for a few moments. The woman peered across the cafeteria to gaze at Noelle, then she smiled and nodded, saying something which made Per laugh. He carried coffee on a tray to the table Noelle had chosen. 'I have just been told,' he said, 'that I have good taste in English girls. It's all right,' he pushed a cup towards her, 'I didn't tell her you were one of my employees. I said you were a family friend. Are you pleased with me for saying that?' he asked with a slanting smile.

She was, of course, but she was not prepared to tell him so. They sipped the coffee and Noelle gazed round at the modern interior. Again it was built mainly of wood – the walls, the floor, the self-service counter. It was indeed a country of wood. There was an abundance of it everywhere.

Per asked, 'Your parents – you live with them?'

'Only during college vacations,' she told him. 'Before I qualified, I lived in digs in London, like Kirsten. My parents live in Wiltshire.'

'Isn't that the county of Stonehenge?' He smiled. 'You see, I know something about the history of your country. I must come and visit that great stone circle some day. Maybe I would see you wandering about the countryside.'

Noelle laughed to hide the quick thrill of pleasure at the thought of meeting Per Arneson on her home territory.

'Tell me more about your family,' he encouraged. 'Now you're wondering why. Well, we must have something to talk about, mustn't we?'

He was using his charm to good purpose because she felt her tenseness ebbing away. Her father, she told him, was an assistant bank manager, her mother a housewife. 'All very respectable,' she added, with a smile.

'And you live a blameless life, like your parents?'

Something inside her tightened again. 'I live the sort of life I want to lead.'

He laughed. 'In other words, it's none of my business. So you give me an evasive answer, intending either to snub me or to stimulate my interest.'

'Suppose,' she challenged, 'I were to ask if *you* lived a blameless life? You would tell me it was not my business, wouldn't you?'

'No.' His eyes held hers in a curiously compelling fashion. 'I would tell you the truth. I would say that I did not lead a blameless life. Does it worry you?'

With a great effort, she detached her gaze from his. She forced a shrug. 'Why should it? It's your life. Our paths are only crossing for a month or two, aren't they? When I leave Norway, I doubt if I shall ever see you again.'

The words, as she spoke them, sounded like a tolling bell, and her mind began to mourn as though someone – or something – had died even as it struggled to be born.

'My dear Noelle,' his voice came softly, 'why so morbid? The world, after all, is not so big. We might well meet again – if we wished it.'

She shook her head with the vigour of a child responding to someone who was asking her to do something she knew to be wrong. 'There wouldn't be any point in our meeting again. I'm not your type. I don't succumb, like all the other women in your life, to your charm, do I?' It was lucky, she told herself, that he could not see into the secret places of her mind. 'And you certainly wouldn't fit into my world.' She scraped back her chair.

He followed her to the door and they went outside without speaking. As they passed the shop where she had admired the coats and sweaters, he caught her arm and propelled her into the shop. He went up to the counter, selected a woollen garment, held it up and said, 'This was the one, wasn't it?'

Noelle stared. 'Yes, but—'

'You shall have it.' He paid, the sweater was wrapped and he put the parcel into her arms. 'Now, you must not refuse. It would be an insult. It is – shall we say – a "good-bye" present. After your sad little soliloquy back there in the cafeteria, I could not bear you to go away without a reminder of me!' He was laughing at her now. Instead of thanking him she turned away. 'No, no,' he said, pretending to be worried, 'don't throw it at me – unless you attach yourself to it, too.'

She did not know why his action had hurt so much. Was it the easy way he had accepted all she had said, without trying to disprove it? Well, it was true, she was not his type, and he had no place in her kind of life. *So what was the matter with her?* At last she managed to thank him and he accepted her thanks with a mocking bow.

'To you the price was so high, to me so low.' Which, Noelle thought bitterly, just about summed up their different – and irreconcilable – situations.

When Noelle returned to her room, she removed the sweater from the package and pressed it to her face. It was the softness, she told herself firmly, that had made her do it, no other reason. She held it against her, admiring its colours, then with reluctance put it on the bed.

The girls on duty in the dining-room stood in a group, waiting for the first diners to take their places. Noelle was busier than ever that evening. Three of her four tables had been occupied for some time when the fourth, the *di-rektör*'s table came into use. As he approached it, Noelle saw that he was not alone. Preceding him was Sonja Linde.

Sonja did not go straight to the table. She stopped now and then to chat to the guests, many of whom knew her as a result of their patronage of the bar. As Sonja talked in German, French, Danish and Dutch, Per stood smiling by her side. Yes, Noelle thought with a strange and uncontrollable stab of pain, Sonja would make him an ideal wife. She had the poise, the grooming, the right social and educational background.

Now and then Per would join in the conversation in whatever language his guests – and his girl-friend – happened to be speaking and Noelle realized with an odd pang what an accomplished man he was. They looked so right together, he and Sonja, Noelle thought unhappily, that she was convinced Per Arneson intended eventually to marry the girl at his side.

She had the feeling that during the walk that afternoon, and in all his dealings with her, Noelle, he had been playing with her as a kitten plays with a ball of wool – pulling her, patting her, pushing her this way and that, just to see how far and in which direction she would run, knowing all the time that he had complete control over her movements. That he could unwind her completely if he chose, entangling her utterly and inescapably with himself.

Per lifted his head and caught her watching him, and an eyebrow rose in a silent question. Then he smiled and at that moment Sonja glanced at him. Her eyes followed the line of his smile and came up against Noelle. For a few seconds, Sonja's expression twisted with hate. Certainly Per had not seen it, because he motioned his guest to her seat with an unworried smile.

At the table Sonja picked up the menu, but instead of studying it, held it up to her face and gazed at him over the top of it, trying to seduce him with her eyes. He laughed at her playfulness and took up his own menu. Noelle waited a few moments, then, hoping she had judged the time lapse correctly, approached the table.

Sonja frowned up at her. 'Go away,' she said petulantly. 'It's much too soon. You haven't given us time to make up our minds, has she, Per?'

He put down his copy of the menu. 'I have made up my mind, Sonja, but,' to Noelle, 'return in a few moments, please.'

Was there, Noelle wondered, inexplicably over-senstive to his reactions, the slightest reprimand in his tone? She withdrew and continued with her work of waiting on the other guests. When at last she was free to attend at the *direktör*'s table, Sonja said, 'Now you have left it too long. Why did you not come back sooner?'

Noelle stammered, 'I'm – I'm sorry. I've been busy with other guests—'

'We are more important than the other guests, are we not, Per? You are the owner, after all.'

Per said, ignoring his companion's outburst, 'The order, Miss Roberts, have you forgotten?'

'Forgotten, Herr Arneson?' Noelle felt she could take so much, but no more. 'Of course not, but I have other tables to—' Per's raised eyebrows, over ice-cold eyes, brought the sentence to an untimely end. Haltingly Noelle apologized and was forced to meet Sonja's gloating smile as she began to give her order.

A little later, Noelle was placing soup plates in front of Per and Sonja, preparatory to filling them, when Sonja said, 'This girl is so slow, Per. Why do we not have one of the others waiting on us? She is so hopeless she's spoiling my enjoyment.'

Per said nothing, and Noelle hated him for his silence. Why didn't he reprimand his girl-friend for her rudeness as he so often reprimanded her, Noelle?

She carried the container of soup from the trolley and started to ladle it into Sonja's plate. Sonja's arm lifted so swiftly that Noelle hardly knew it had happened. The contents of the ladle were thrown in all directions. Some of the brown liquid dropped on to the tablecloth, some on to Sonja's skirt, and yet more down Noelle's crisp, white apron.

Sonja gave a little high-pitched shriek. 'Oh, oh, now look what she has done, this girl! Per, you must fire her, you must—'

'It wasn't my fault,' Noelle blurted out. 'You moved your arm deliberately . . .'

'*Miss Roberts!*' Per, tight-lipped, was standing now.

'But it's true, Herr Arneson, she—'

'Will you be quiet, Miss Roberts!'

The attention of the roomful of guests was firmly fixed on the play which was being enacted at the owner's table.

The *hovmester*, the head waiter, came rushing forward, shaking his head, his words placating. 'I am so sorry, Fröken Linde. It was a terrible thing to happen. Your dress . . . She is so careless sometimes, this young lady Fröken Roberts. I have had good reason to complain now and then to her before . . .'

Noelle stared at him. It wasn't true, it simply wasn't true! How could everyone let her down like this, even Herr Krüger, kindly though he usually was?

'But, Herr Krüger,' Noelle pleaded, 'I didn't do it. It was Fröken Linde . . .'

'Fröken Roberts!' Olaf Krüger cried. 'You must come with me, you really must come—'

'Wait, Olaf,' Per Arneson said. 'Find another girl to take over these four tables temporarily. Miss Roberts,' he pushed back his chair, 'come with me. Sonja,' with a brief bow, 'please excuse me. I shall not be long.'

'Dismiss her,' said Sonja, 'she's no good. She has ruined my dress! Look at it . . .'

In Per's office behind the reception desk, he faced her, but before he could speak Noelle said, 'Please believe me, Herr Arneson, it *wasn't* my fault. Fröken Linde jerked my hand – deliberately. And it's not true what Herr Krüger said, he hasn't had complaints about me before. He must have been confusing me with someone else.'

'You,' his eyes sparkled with anger like ice in the winter sun, 'are calling two of my best and most trusted employees liars? You, a complete and untried newcomer to my staff, totally inexperienced in the work until I took you on, are asking me to believe your word against theirs?' He raised his voice. 'Do you take me for a *fool*, Miss Roberts?'

The tears came trickling through, she could not stop them. Helplessly she shook her head. 'It wasn't my fault, Herr Arneson, it wasn't my fault . . .'

Her voice trailed into the silence, the tears kept coming. Then Per said, 'A lesson you will have to learn, if you wish to keep your place in this establishment, is that even if an accusation made against you is not true,' she looked up quickly, hopefully, but it was plain he still had not believed her, 'you must not say so. The hotel guest, like the customer, is always right. Any attempt you may make to defend yourself will inevitably be regarded by them as insolence. You will have to apologize to Fröken Linde.'

Noelle stared. '*Apologize?* For something I didn't do? No, I can't, I just can't do—'

'You will apologize, Miss Roberts. If you wish to stay, you must accept the discipline of the hotel. And you must accept orders from those above you. Do you understand?'

For a long time she stared at the damp, crumpled handkerchief in her hand. If she agreed, her pride would take a cruel blow. If she refused, she would never see this man again.

At last she raised her head. 'I'll apologize.'

His face expressionless, he motioned her to the door. When she stood at Sonja's side, hands clasped, head down, muttering her words of apology, the smile that spread across

Sonja's face was a mixture of crowing triumph and sadistic pleasure. Per could not have missed it, because it was still on her face as she looked at him. Now whom did he believe? Now was he able to judge who was telling the truth?

He resumed his seat at the table. 'Get on with your work, Miss Roberts,' was all he said.

Word went round the domestic quarters next morning that the owner had gone away.

'To Trondheim,' they said, 'to one of his other hotels.'

Noelle felt an unaccountable sense of loss, and then told herself wearily how stupid she was to feel that way. Per Arneson might now and then for his sister's sake adopt a friendly attitude towards her, but deep down, he regarded her as just another employee. After all, look how he had treated her last night while she was on duty. If he had had any real friendliness in him at all, he would at least have called Sonja into his room so that she, Noelle, could have apologized in private, instead of suffering the humiliation of having to do so in front of a roomful of guests. Although a small protesting voice inside her said he would have acted in the same way towards any difficult employee, and he could not make an exception of her . . .

Now he had gone away. For how long? Noelle wondered. She asked Kirsten when they met that afternoon. For two or three days, who could tell, Kirsten said.

'What happened,' Kirsten asked, 'at dinner yesterday evening? Per came in in a filthy mood and I couldn't get a civil word out of him the whole evening.'

Noelle explained. 'But Per wouldn't believe I wasn't responsible for the accident. He wouldn't listen when I tried to tell him it was Sonja's fault.'

Kirsten said disgustedly, 'My brother knows his woman well enough to realize what a cat she can be, especially towards the so-called "lower" members of staff. Especially,' looking up from her sewing, 'when that member of staff has everything she's got and more.' Noelle shook her head modestly. 'But you have, you know, and you're so much sweeter and consequently more attractive with it. And if my brother weren't so stupid about her, if he were not so fooled by her cleverness with languages and her smooth manner with the guests, he would see her for what she really is – cheap, vicious and vindictive.'

Noelle sighed. 'Well, he accepted her word over mine last night. He absolutely refused to believe what I said.' Momentarily her lip quivered. 'He was really nasty.'

Kirsten reached out and patted Noelle's back. 'I'll talk to him. I'll make him believe you.'

'Thanks, Kirsten, but don't bother. It wouldn't do any good now. The sooner the incident is forgotten the better.'

But Noelle could not forget, not even when she saw Per's table standing empty that evening at dinner. She kept thinking she could see him walking into the dining-room, or that she could hear his voice out in the entrance foyer. But of course he never came.

Per was away for longer than the two or three days that his sister had estimated. During his absence, Noelle had a free day and she and Kirsten hired bicycles from a local shop – it was common practice, Kirsten said, for shops to hire out bicycles to tourists in the holiday season – and went on a long cycle ride, puffing up the hills, racing down them, hair flying free. Noelle was daunted by the hair-raisingly steep hairpin bends. But Kirsten tackled them with a grin while Noelle dismounted and pushed her bicycle round, keeping a careful distance between herself and the precipitous drop at the side of the road.

In the evenings, Noelle went for walks with Mark Anderson. He had started to kiss her good night, and she did not repel him, although she did not enjoy it. His kisses were hesitant and he usually chose to kiss her in the full glare of the hotel lights, while cars were arriving and leaving and music from the dancing escaped through the swing doors.

One evening, about ten days after Per had gone away, Kirsten persuaded Noelle to join the dancing in the 'cellar'.

It was not really a cellar, she explained, because the hotel was modern. It was a large room which had been built on a lower level than the rest of the building.

Noelle protested that she was a member of staff and therefore should not join the activities which were really intended for the guests. Kirsten assured her that, as long as a member of staff was off duty, it was allowed. 'We're a democratic country,' she had added, smiling. 'We believe in democracy and we put it into practice.'

So Noelle put on a skirt and pulled over her head the sweater which Per had given her. It was the first time she had worn it and, looking at her reflection, she realized how much it suited her. It certainly did not hide the shapely outline. It also emphasized the rich brown of her hair.

The 'cellar' was candlelit and mysterious shadows moved over the walls. In an alcove a young man played an organ softly while the dancers rested. In the semi-darkness people drank and smoked, and the talk was in many languages.

As Noelle stood at the top of the short flight of steps which led down into the room, Kirsten saw her and raised her hand in greeting. A little shyly, Noelle joined the group of men who surrounded her friend and Kirsten made sketchy introductions. Most of the young men, Noelle guessed, were Norwegian, but all of them could speak English.

'We are taught it at school,' one of them explained. 'And of course many of us visit England during our college vacations. It is not, after all, so very far away!'

Another asked, 'You like our country?'

'I haven't seen a great deal of it,' Noelle had to admit, 'but what I have seen is beautiful beyond my expectations.'

Two or three of the young men pounded each other on their backs in an orgy of self-congratulation, making Noelle laugh. 'And the people – you like us?'

'Very much indeed,' Noelle told them with complete honesty. 'In many ways you're so like us I feel quite at home.

You're so understanding, so polite, so kind to visitors—'

The young men laughed and one said, '*You* are a visitor, therefore you see only our virtues, not our vices. We have them, you know. We smoke a lot, we drink a lot, we—'

Someone clamped a hand over his mouth. 'Don't go on, Knut. We all know what you are going to say!'

The organ began to play again and Knut said, 'That is Kjell providing the music. He plays it every night during the holiday season. Of course, he does not do it for nothing! Come and dance, Noelle?'

So Noelle danced opposite Knut, not quite able to abandon herself to the rhythm of the music as he was doing, but at his words of encouragement, came near to it. When the dance was over, he saw some friends across the room and with an apology and a bow, left her. She could have joined Kirsten's group again, but she would have had to push her way through the crowd to reach her friend's side, so she looked around for a dark corner – the darkest she could find – and retired into it.

It was in an alcove and there was a bench seat. From there Noelle found she could watch without herself being seen. Or so she thought until someone came to stand in front of her. A glass was being offered to her and a familiar voice spoke, a voice which made her heart nearly stop with – what? Fear? Dismay? Or – joy?

Noelle accepted the glass – she could not very well refuse – but she could find nothing to say. Even if she had, she doubted if she could have got the words out. The materialization of the man who had been so much in her mind during his absence it was almost as if he had never been away had momentarily deprived her mind of thoughts and her lungs of the breath necessary to give voice to them.

'You have been getting on well with my fellow-countrymen. You dance well, Miss Roberts.'

Per's voice, holding a challenge, brought her to life. She looked up at him. 'How long have you been here?'

'Since before you came in. I, too, lurk in dark corners

when I choose.'

She asked, simply for something to say, 'When did you get back?'

'This evening. I dined in my apartment.' He held up his glass. 'Come, Miss Roberts, let us drink to my return.' Her glass did not rise with his. 'Or,' sardonically, 'would you rather change the toast to the shortness of my stay, to my speedy departure?'

Suppose she told him she never wanted him to go away again? He would laugh, no doubt, congratulate himself that yet another woman was running towards him. That he would run towards her, too, she also had no doubt. Had he not told her that, where women were concerned, he never did otherwise?

Yes, she raised her glass, she would drink to his return, but he would never know with how much pleasure she did so.

He moved nearer, standing so close in front of her his knees touched hers, and she experienced the feel of him creeping up her limbs like the sudden warmth of a fire on a freezing day. In his cream jacket and black open-necked shirt, with his towering height and the honey-gold of his hair, with the near-darkness of the room adding a ruthless, devastating attraction to his handsome features, he looked, every particle of him, the Viking his distant ancestors had been.

Give him a willing woman, Noelle thought, and he would pillage and plunder, robbing her of all she was capable of giving, and more beyond that, leaving her ransacked and destitute of all pride and self-respect. Then he would pass on to the next . . . and the next . . .

She could not see his expression as he looked down at her. His face was in shadow, although with the glow of the candlelit room behind him his profile was thrown large and menacing on to the walls of the alcove.

His voice came low and smoothly seductive. 'Have you forgiven me?' Noelle frowned. 'You can't remember? That, in itself, is a good sign. Should I remind you?'

'For the unfeeling way you treated me over that incident with Fröken Linde?'

'You put it a little – shall we say – impudently? But yes, I mean that.'

Delaying her answer deliberately, Noelle drained her glass, placing it on a nearby table. Her face lifted and she said slowly, 'No, I haven't forgiven you. I doubt if I ever will. You ground my pride into the dust, so how could I—?'

A gasp replaced the words she had been about to speak. Her whole body jerked and jarred as a hand came out, gripped her wrist and pulled her up against the human wall of rock that stood in front of her. His lips, parting hers, had her head forced back until she thought her neck would break. She could not struggle and say, 'People will see us', because they were in almost total darkness. She could not struggle at all because his hold on her arms was like a vice, so tight she was convinced that if he did not let her go soon, it would dam the circulation of her blood.

But he did let her go, saying through his teeth, 'No woman speaks to me like that and gets away without retaliation.'

Noelle sank on to the bench, putting a shaking hand to her hair. 'You're quite unfair! You – you change roles to suit your mood. You approach as a – a man, the brother of my friend, and like a flash of lightning you change into a vicious demon of an employer.'

Instead of becoming annoyed at her accusation, he seemed amused. 'Surely your description is a little off-course? Since when has an employer seized a member of his staff as I seized you? Shouldn't the word have been – lover?' He ran a hand through his hair. 'And while we're on the subject, if you don't like me as an employer, you know what you can do, don't you?' The music changed to a sweeter sound and his mood changed with it. His hand reached out. 'Dance with me?'

Noelle asked, with a small, provocative smile, 'Which are you now? Was that an order from my boss, or an invitation from my friend's brother?'

The thumbs on her wrist rubbed round and round caressingly. He said softly, 'Now that depends on you. If you're going to be perverse, I shall have to order you, as your employer. If you're compliant and docile, I shall ask you as a family friend.'

She stood and placed herself in front of him. His arms went round her and he moved her from their dark corner on to the dance floor.

He said, 'I see you're wearing the sweater I bought you. Surely that must mean something.'

She smiled – she could afford to be happy now she was in his arms – and replied, 'Only that, although you gave it to me, I liked it so much I couldn't resist wearing it.'

He pretended to wince at her frank reply. 'Don't you find it a little warm in this close atmosphere? A woollen garment like that is intended for below-zero winter days.'

Noelle shook her head. 'I'm wearing very little underneath it.' Immediately the words were spoken she regretted them.

His interest was immediate. 'Oh?' His hand moved down and found the ribbed edge of the sweater, slipping underneath the woollen fabric. His outspread palm exploring the flesh of her back made her shiver and burn at the same time.

'Per,' she whispered, 'please don't.'

'Why,' he whispered back, his lips against her ear, 'don't you like it?'

She did not answer. How could she when she really wanted to say, It's so wonderful having you touch me I don't want you to stop.

She said desperately, her legs barely able to move to the music, 'Per, what are you trying to do?'

'I should have thought, my sweet, it was obvious what I was trying to do. There was a certain – promise in the kiss we have just exchanged. You must surely have felt it yourself. I should like to follow it up and go wherever it leads. You are sleeping in my room. There's room for two—'

She jerked away, putting her hands behind her and tugging at his hand which was moving so softly, so expertly, over her shoulder blades, 'Your sister said that she's always admired your technique. Well, Herr Arneson, I don't. I intend to be one of the few who slips through your net!'

She pushed her way through the dancers, ran up the steps and out of the cellar, into the bright, dazzling lights of the hotel. In her room – Per's room – she turned the key and threw herself, shaking with anger and disappointment, on to the bed.

As she lay there fighting for breath and rationality, she was forced to acknowledge that the net – Per's net – had been closing round her since the day they had met. Now it had closed completely. She might flounder and fight, but he had caught her, and there was no escape.

CHAPTER FIVE

FOR the next two days Noelle did not see Per. He was busy, Kirsten said. All his meals were being served in his flat. She invited Noelle to join her that evening. She was fed up with her brother's company, she complained. He was like a prowling lion, liable at any moment to break out into a roar and frighten his little sister away!

But Noelle refused. She had promised, she lied, to go walking with Mark Anderson. To prove to Kirsten – and herself – that she was right, she sought Mark out in the kitchen and asked if he would go with her that evening. He seemed pleased at her invitation and Noelle hoped he would not read into it more than she intended. They watched the sun sink below the mountains, leaving behind a golden mist.

On their return, as they approached the hotel, walking into the light which was beaming from its uncurtained windows, Mark stopped and kissed her. Feeling that it would be unfair to resist since she had, after all, invited him to accompany her, Noelle allowed his kisses. He drew her close, closer than usual, and continued to hold her, no matter how many cars arrived and car doors slammed.

His kissing grew more passionate and the thought drifted into Noelle's mind that he chose to show his feelings for her in such a public place as an odd form of exhibitionism. Normally a quiet, rather timid person, perhaps he wanted to prove to the world that he too was a man, with manly feelings.

A car drew up, sweeping into park and braking violently. It had driven so near to them they had jumped. As they drew apart, Noelle had the crazy idea that the driver, if he had dared, would have run them down.

With Mark's arm round her, she watched Per Arneson

throw open the car door and get out. He gave Noelle a shrivelling look. To her dismay he approached.

'Forgive the interruption,' he said sarcastically, 'but there is something in my room in the staff house that I require, Miss Roberts. To save me the trouble of going to my apartment first, may I borrow your key?'

His voice was curt and although the request was phrased as a question, it was really a command. Noelle felt in her pocket and held out the key, which Per took with brief thanks. She watched him stride across the road and decided to wait until he returned to avoid meeting him. But Mark started to kiss her again, and she came to the conclusion that the lesser of the two evils would be to go to her room and risk coming face to face with her employer. It was possible, anyway, that while Mark had been kissing her, she had missed Per. He had probably found what he wanted and gone into the hotel, leaving her key in the room and the door unlocked.

But to her dismay, she discovered he was still there. He was sitting on the bed looking through a pile of papers. He looked up sharply as she entered, but he did not speak. Noelle murmured that she was sorry to intrude but thought he had gone. Still he said nothing and she felt acutely embarrassed by his silence. She picked up a comb from the dressing-table and ran it through her hair. Then she wandered to the window and looked across at the dark shape of the hotel, still streaming with lights.

While he was in the room she could not prepare for bed, she could not even sit down because his presence disturbed her so deeply. As soon as she had pulled the curtains, she regretted the action. It made the situation so much more intimate. At last she sat down, clasping her hands.

Having apparently found what he was looking for, Per collected the papers, pushed them back into the cupboard and locked it, slipping the key into his pocket. He stood in front of her holding out the key to the room. As she took it, she looked up a little tremulously. He seemed angry. Had he not forgiven her for what she had said to him that evening in the cellar? But it seemed there was something else on his mind.

'I should be obliged,' he said, his eyes hard, 'if the next time you and your English boy-friend,' Noelle winced at the word 'English', guessing he had used it deliberately to drive the wedge of differing nationalities between them, 'feel like making love, that you do it either in private, or at some distance from the hotel environs. You are not my guests, you are my employees, and as such, I expect you to conduct yourselves with reasonable dignity and a little more restraint when in sight of the hotel patrons.'

He turned at the door, adding, with deep cynicism, 'The kind of restraint you showed the other evening, so obviously hypocritical, when I made a certain – suggestion. I had even begun to believe you were sincere in your objection to what I had said. I should have known a woman better than that. What she says and what she does are always a world apart. And you are no exception.'

At dinner the following evening, Per entertained Sonja Linde again. Her skirt was long and the material of the top was more noticeable by its absence than its presence. She had outdressed all the other women guests, but with her panache and beauty, she carried it off so well it did not seem out of place.

Remembering the last time she had served Sonja, Noelle grew nervous. She must be on her guard, she told herself. There must not be another accident at the *direktör*'s table. Per gave Noelle the order curtly, without even looking up. This in itself, she felt, was a rebuke, although what she had done to deserve it, she could not guess.

This time, while serving the soup course, Noelle kept a careful watch on Sonja's movements. All went well. Then came the main course and Noelle maintained her watch, but Sonja merely looked at her with irritation as if incensed by her slowness. Noelle refused to hurry, however. It was imperative that she should do nothing wrong. But she did do something wrong. It happened while she was serving Sonja's host.

As she stood at Per's side, she was overpoweringly aware of his nearness and her nervousness returned. She handled the vegetables awkwardly and to her dismay the serving spoon slipped. Per's hand shot out to steady hers, but he was too late to save the situation. A large quantity of beans was flung across the tablecloth, staining its clinical whiteness into a dull, damp green.

Turning pale – this, she thought, must be the end – she waited for the explosion of anger. Per looked up into her face, a deep frown furrowing his brow. He must have seen her dismay, because the frown disappeared, to be replaced by a reproving shake of the head.

Sonja tutted and spoke complainingly in her native tongue, but Per replied in English, whether out of politeness to Noelle, or whether to annoy her, Noelle could never afterwards decide.

'My dear Sonja,' Per drawled, 'you have to make allowances. Miss Roberts is a total amateur in the subtle art of waiting at table. Her true vocation, like my sister's, is dress design. When have you ever known a graduate in dress design be an expert at conveying food from a dish in her hand to a dish on the table?'

'You are paying her as a waitress,' Sonja snapped, adding disgustedly, 'The girl should be fired. You're wasting your money.'

Per replied carelessly, 'I have plenty to waste, even if I am fool enough to waste it on an inexperienced, untrained, rather clumsy friend of my sister's.' The smile he lifted to Noelle was touched with derision. He waved his hand towards the mess on the table. 'Hadn't you better do something about this, Miss Roberts?'

Her relief at his tolerant attitude made her overlook his sarcasm at her expense, and she became uncharacteristically effusive in her apologies. Sonja smirked and Per raised his eyebrows. 'There's no need to go on, Miss Roberts,' he said.

'I've forgiven you.' He caught the eye of the head waiter who hurried over, shaking his head when he saw the mess. He gave Noelle a reproachful frown and in a few moments the *direktör*'s table was cleared, the cloth replaced and the cutlery reset.

'Shall I change the waitress, Herr Arneson?' Olaf Krüger asked. 'I should never have given you such an inexperienced newcomer.'

But Per shook his head. 'Carry on, Miss Roberts,' he directed long-sufferingly. 'Try not to let it happen again.'

When Per and his guest went into the lounge for coffee, Noelle sighed with relief. When Kirsten appeared to take her place at her brother's table, Noelle sighed again – with pleasure. Kirsten would present no problem, and ironically, Noelle found herself so relaxed in waiting on her friend, she served every course without a single mistake.

Kirsten said, 'You're an excellent waitress. I don't know what Per is grumbling about.'

Noelle's heart sank. So the *direktör* had been complaining about her. How much longer, she wondered, would he tolerate her on his staff?

'Can you spare a moment?' Kirsten asked. Noelle said just a second or two. 'Tomorrow afternoon a trip along the fjords has been organized on a motor ship Per owns. A number of the guests here are going. Would you like to come?'

Noelle said that unfortunately she was on duty, but otherwise it would have been wonderful.

'I'll get you the afternoon off. Per will arrange it. The *hovmester*, Herr Krüger, can't refuse him. After all, Per's the boss.'

'But I don't think you'll get Per to agree. He's not very pleased with me at the moment. Anyway, it would hardly be fair to the others, would it?'

Kirsten waved her objections aside. 'You can make the time up another day. Be ready tomorrow immediately after lunch. As soon as I've finished my meal here, I'll find Per.

Don't worry, I'll talk my brother round.'

It seemed that Kirsten was as good as her word, because the head waiter informed Noelle when she arrived for work next day that she had been given the afternoon off, at the special request of the *direktör*. Olaf Krüger looked at her a little curiously, and it did not take Noelle long to realize just what he was thinking.

It was warm and sunny as the crowd awaited the arrival of the motor ship which was to take them on their journey. Kirsten got out of Per's car and pushed her way to Noelle's side.

They greeted each other and Noelle asked, 'Am I dressed appropriately?' She was wearing the sweater Per had given her, with rust-coloured pants which echoed one of the colours in the sweater. Over it all she wore a short suede jacket to match the trousers.

'Just right,' Kirsten said. 'So you've treated yourself to one of our woollen sweaters?'

At that moment Per joined them, nodding briefly at Noelle.

'Well,' Noelle said to Kirsten, 'I – I didn't buy it.'

Kirsten asked, intrigued, 'Then who did?' Involuntarily, Noelle glanced at the man beside her. Kirsten said, eyes wide, 'Not Per?' Her gaze swung to her brother. 'Per, is it true?'

'That sweater?' He shrugged. 'In a moment of weakness. What of it? It was no great hardship to me to part with a fraction of my money to give the impoverished friend of my sister something she was obviously longing to have.'

Thus lightly he dismissed the giving of something Noelle had grown strangely to treasure.

Kirsten's eyes gleamed. 'That was a long explanation, *kjære bror*, for such a simple little act of charity. Are you sure you were not motivated by something else? Was it perhaps part of your persuasive tactics?'

Per seemed annoyed. 'Be quiet, *lille söster*. Run away and play.'

The motor ship came from its moorings and drew alongside the jetty. Painted in white across the blue hull were the words, '*m/s Kirsten*, Hotel Arneson.'

'Yes,' said Kirsten, 'my brother thought enough of me once to name his motor ship after me.' She said the words a little plaintively, intending to draw a response from the man of whom she spoke.

He smiled without speaking, bunching his hand into a fist and pushing it playfully towards her chin. To Noelle, the act turned him for a few breath-robbing moments into a human being with affection, warmth and feeling. Gone was the customary arrogance which moulded his features into remoteness, blotting out compassion. There was a passing softness in his eyes which made the blood cascade in her veins. When, for a fleeting second, he moved that look from Kirsten to her, Noelle's heart leapt like a newborn lamb. And when he looked away, she felt as lost as a lamb searching for its mother.

The ship had docked, the gangway was lowered. Per was the first to step on board, disappearing at once up some narrow stairs and into the captain's cabin.

Noelle commented, with surprise, 'Per's coming with us?'

'Today, yes, although he does not often come. When he does, he speaks the commentary, telling the passengers about the places we are passing, and so on. He's a fluent linguist.'

As soon as all the passengers had embarked, the ship cast off. There was a sundeck and below, in the area equipped as a lounge, there was a small counter at which food and hot drinks were dispensed. There were seats on the sundeck and the Norwegian flag fluttered from a mast. As the ship moved out into the open fjord, Noelle stood at the rail and revelled in the beauty around her.

The pine-clad hills sloped steeply to the water's edge. Ahead the rugged mountains closed in, forming a rocky barrier to all progress – or so it seemed until the ship moved on, to find that there were no mountain barriers after all, that it was an illusion and the gaps ahead that had seemed so narrow were in reality very wide. The sunlight caught the tops of the mountains, revealing rushing torrents of water plunging down the hillsides in froth and foam.

Here and there a house or cottage perched on rocks just above the fjord. How, Noelle wondered, did the owners reach their homes? The paths were so narrow and so steep, it made her feel out of breath just looking at them.

A voice coming over the loudspeakers made her tingle, speeding her heartbeats, blotting out the beauty her eyes were seeing, in an effort to visualize the man who was speaking. If, she thought with despair, the sound of his voice does this to me, what would I feel if he touched me . . .?

Some of these villages they were passing, Per was saying, were, in a sense, isolated and cut off. There were no roads leading to them, he said, and they were accessible only by boat along the fjord. The ferries would call at some of these villages, taking on passengers or landing them. Although isolated, the villagers were not lonely, because they enjoyed a happy social life.

Per switched effortlessly from English to French, from French to German, and after that, to Dutch. Whatever the language he was speaking, Noelle listened simply because she could not help it. His voice was a magnet and although she could not understand a word, it gave her almost physical pleasure to listen to him.

She glanced over her shoulder, wondering where Kirsten was, and found her talking animatedly to two young men. Noelle wondered, smiling to herself, if Kirsten was ever left quite alone by the opposite sex. It was an attribute Kirsten shared with her brother, a family characteristic, perhaps. She found herself wondering about Kirsten and Per's parents. Beyond the fact that they lived in Oslo, she knew little about them.

Feeling Noelle's glance, Kirsten waved and, with a smile, left the young men. 'Hi,' she said, 'all alone?'

'But not lonely,' Noelle smiled. 'I was just thinking,' she looked along the fjord at the steep slope of the mountains, 'what a clever brother you've got.' At Kirsten's puzzled frown, she explained, 'The way he changes so easily from one language to another. The way he speaks them all as if he were born in that particular country.'

Kirsten laughed. 'He should be good. He read languages at university. He intended becoming an interpreter at a very high level.'

'Then why—?' Noelle's hand moved, encompassing the ship and including by implication the hotels Per owned and his role in running them.

Kirsten understood what she was trying to say. 'The hotels belonged to my father, but he retired comparatively young, wishing to enjoy the money he had accumulated. Per took over the properties and the responsibilities from him. But it was Per who expanded the business to include a ship or two, and an interest in hotels in other countries. There are even one or two in England, which is how we came to travel with him in the first place. He had been attending to his business interests for a few weeks and delayed his departure so that he could sail with me – and you. Except,' she smiled impishly, 'that when I told him I would have a girl-friend with me, he groaned even louder. I don't know what he expected to see when you appeared.'

Noelle made a face. 'He made it plain from the start that he didn't approve of me.'

Kirsten looked at her, smiling slowly, but she said nothing. Then another passenger called her name and she left, saying she would soon be back. So for a while Noelle was alone again. When someone came to stand beside her, she assumed it was Kirsten and did not turn. But when that person's arm moved closer to hers and that person's shoulder pressed against her shoulder, she frowned and looked round – only to feel her pulses leap, and sudden colour sting her cheeks.

Per smiled and his eyes held a touch of intimacy, but he

Best Seller Romance
FOOD FOR LOVE
Rachel Lindsay

did not speak. Noelle felt compelled to break the silence. 'I – I liked your commentary.'

Now there was a faint mockery lurking in the smile. 'You understood it? Every word?'

'Unfortunately, no. The English, of course – that was near-perfect,' Per's head inclined ironically, 'and here and there, the French, but the rest—' She shook her head. 'I'm afraid I'm no expert at languages.'

'But then,' with another smile, and his eyes, so near, seemed to linger on the shape of her lips, 'I am no expert at dress design. Each to his own. That's the saying, is it not?'

Noelle smiled back at him, her colour still high, her features animated because of his nearness. After a few moments, he removed his eyes from her and stared out over the fjord. 'You like what you've seen of my country?'

'I've been breathing it into my system and it's now circulating in my veins.'

'In other words,' a brief glance at her, 'you've taken it to your heart?'

'Completely.'

'And its people?'

Her hand touched her body in the region of her heart. 'They're here, too.'

'Male and female alike? You make no exceptions?'

Her confusion must have shown, because he laughed aloud. 'So I nearly tricked you into telling me whether I had a place, even an infinitesimal one, in your heart!' His arm came to rest round her waist. 'I've kissed you once, I've kissed you twice. Tell me, Noelle, if I kissed you again – and perhaps again, would you begin to soften towards me, give a little, and then perhaps a little more . . .'

As he spoke, Noelle was shaking her head vigorously. She wished she could shake off the feelings the touch of his chest against her shoulder provoked. 'I have every intention,' she told him, 'of proving to you that your technique, as Kirsten called it, is not foolproof. Thus,' she smiled, 'helping Kirsten to win the bet she had with you about me.'

He laughed. 'You're wasting your time, you know. Shall I tell you something?' The arm around her tightened. 'The more a woman runs from me, the more I run after her.'

Noelle smiled, not with amusement, more with a kind of ruffled confusion. 'You said once that women ran after *you*, with their arms open wide, just waiting for you to run into them.'

'Ah, but there is always the odd one who is – shall we say – a little difficult.' His eyes baited her. 'It's the obstinate ones who present a challenge, an irresistible challenge, and who make life so much more interesting.'

'Suppose,' she spoke carefully, 'suppose one of the "difficult" ones is absolutely determined to escape?' She was not, she told herself firmly, talking about herself. After all, she was not involved in any way with this man beside her, except as employer to employee. Her link with him through Kirsten was so slender it meant nothing.

'She doesn't escape,' he answered simply. 'You see,' his face was so near she could smell the faint masculine fragrance of lotion on his skin, 'I always corner them in the end. Then I pounce,' his voice grew gruff and guttural, 'and devour.'

Noelle shifted irritably and Per looked at her, pulling away a little, eyeing her flushed cheeks, the silkiness of her hair lifting in the breeze, the length and breadth of her as she strained to escape from his arm around her waist. 'I wonder,' he murmured, 'what Miss Noelle Roberts tastes like.'

'That's something you'll never know, Herr Arneson.'

'I won't? I assure you,' softly, 'I shall, I shall.'

Kirsten wandered across the deck to join them. 'Yes,' she said, taking in their closeness, 'the arm about the slender waist, the intimate smile, the whisper in the shapely ear – it's all there, dear brother. You're doing your damnedest as usual to get the girl to say "yes", even making her add a pleading "please" just to give you a greater sense of conquest. Is he making progress, Noelle?'

'None at all,' said Noelle quickly, too quickly even to her own ears, and Kirsten's look was questioning.

But Per laughed loudly. 'Alas, it seems I'm up against the traditional English reserve.' His hand slid under Noelle's hair and rested against her neck, his fingers pinching her there a little as if she were a puppy. 'Behold, one of those rare and, today, almost unheard-of species – an un-permissive girl.'

Noelle jerked herself free. His touch aroused emotions so strong they could scarcely be borne. She would not – must not – let this man batter down her defences. That he had already grazed her emotionally, exposing the flesh beneath, she was unable to deny. The mere sight of him, a meeting of their eyes, even the sound of his voice, already had a power over her which frightened her.

Per was called away at that moment, and soon his voice came again over the loudspeaker system. In English he said, 'We hope you are enjoying your trip along one of our beautiful fjords. You may not know that, from the geological point of view, these are sunken valleys, filled by the sea, and because they contain salt water, they never freeze in winter.'

There was a pause, then he continued, 'We are fortunate in Norway in the kind of climate we have. Thanks to the Gulf Stream, which takes tropical water up the Norwegian coast and also warms the air currents, Norway is almost artificially heated. You may not believe it, but the average temperature from June to August in Oslo, our capital city, is higher than, say, San Francisco or London.'

So Per went on talking to his passengers, and Noelle found herself listening, even when he changed to a language she could not understand. She was so absorbed she did not notice that Kirsten had left her again and she was alone. Her eyes lifted to dwell on the great mountains towering above them, a little menacing in their magnificence, awe-inspiring, too, in the way the passage of millions of years had left their message in the jutting overhanging rocks, the great eroded ridges, as if carved with a careless, ruthless hand.

'Have you brought your camera?' Per was beside her again, relaxed, his smile a little mocking. Noelle nodded, her whole metabolism speeded up by the man's proximity. Why, when he came near, did her blood flow more swiftly, her breath come more quickly, her eyes take on a brighter light?

'So you're determined, in your off-duty hours, to behave like a real tourist?' Per rested on his folded arms against the rail. 'Have you, I wonder, noticed that, besides being a country of mountains and fjords, we also have many spectacular waterfalls? And did you know that, by a curious trick of the spray and the sunlight, these waterfalls sometimes form their own rainbows?'

'So if I'm clever with my camera, and quick enough, I might catch a rainbow?'

'Yes, on film. But never,' softly, 'in your hand. A rainbow may be looked at and admired from a distance, like a beautiful, desirable woman, but like that woman, never to be possessed and called your own.'

Noelle looked away, shielding her eyes from the sun which, as the ship turned a little in its course, shone unexpectedly through a gap in the mountains and straight into her eyes. Per Arneson, she reflected, was like a rainbow – elusive, for ever out of reach. He was beside her, but if she stretched out her hand and grasped, there would be nothing there and her hand would return to her side. He would have gone – to some other, more desirable woman. She would never catch a rainbow. She would never 'catch' Per Arneson.

As she gazed over the water, turbulent from the wash of the ship, and watched the brooding mountains, range upon range of them, dominating the sun-dappled fjord in which they dabbled their feet, she became conscious of Per's thoughtful eyes upon her. His expression was wholly serious and her heart jerked in a frightening fashion. She was more disturbed by such a look than if he had been mocking her.

If only he would say something, she thought, smoothing back her wind-blown hair. When he did he said, prosaically, 'Would you like some refreshments? Down below there's a lounge where they serve tea and coffee, sandwiches, if you wish.'

It was a self-service counter and Per told Noelle to find a seat while he collected the coffee. As he carried it on a tray to set it down on the table, he commented,

'We have changed our roles – you at the table, I serving you. How does it feel to be waited on by your employer?'

'Good,' Noelle answered as he sat beside her, offering her the sugar. 'Now I shall become the complaining customer and be rude to you, and you won't be able to answer me back!'

Kirsten, who had come to join them with her own coffee and sandwiches, heard Noelle's response and laughed delightedly. 'She is what the English call "having her own back", Per. Taking her revenge for your unpleasantness when she waits on you at table.'

Per did not seem pleased by his sister's remarks. He looked at Noelle narrowly. 'It's hardly advisable for someone to "take their revenge" on their employer. He might do likewise to her – by showing her the door.'

Noelle concentrated hard on her coffee. 'I meant it in fun, Kirsten,' she murmured a little miserably.

'I know you did,' Kirsten soothed. 'But my brother's sense of humour is somewhat lacking when his precious girl-friend is involved.'

'Leave Sonja out of this,' Per said curtly.

Someone called Kirsten's name and she raised her hand in greeting, picking up her cup. 'Excuse me, please, Noelle. I'm going where my presence is welcome.' She gave her brother a resentful, sisterly look and left them.

Noelle watched her go, wishing she could follow, then she turned to gaze out of the small window at her side, seeing the ruffled surface of the water, the level of which was considerably nearer now they were lower down in the ship.

The view was a little blurred and it was almost as though that water was invading her eyes. There was the swish of the fjord against the sides, the throb of the engine beneath the feet, the smell of burning cigarettes mingling with the coffee, the clinking of crockery and the chatter of the other passengers as they laughed with the girl behind the counter about their confusion over money.

'What's the matter, Noelle?' The question came sharply and startled her.

She tried to find an answer. Per waited and at last she said, 'It's a little – disconcerting the way you jump from, well, friend to – to foe without warning, without even reason.'

'It upsets you?'

Noelle did not reply to the question but said, 'Not that you are my friend, of course. Kirsten's my friend, not you.'

Into the silence, Per said, 'You would like me to be your friend?'

Friend? her heart cried out, and the word rang in her ears. Never that! More than a friend . . . 'No,' she answered.

Per pushed back his chair. 'Please excuse me.' His eyes were cold. 'I am wanted in the captain's cabin.'

Later the ship came within sight of a waterfall. It tumbled, foamed, frothed and roared down the side of a mountain. The spray soaked them as they passed, but the passengers laughed and wiped their faces and their clothes. Everyone, it seemed, had a camera, everyone except people like Per, who had seen it all before.

The motor ship *Kirsten* was by no means the only craft on the fjord. Ferries passed by, some large, bearing cars and lorries, others small, carrying only passengers. The fjord was a busy waterway and, for many, a vital link with the rest of the world.

The captain altered course, turning in the direction of a landing stage which jutted out from the promenade adjoining a group of houses. They clustered together, forming a village which nestled in the shelter of a tree-covered hill. Houses straggled upward, and Noelle supposed there were roads of sorts leading up to them. The houses were all of individual design, some old, red-roofed and tumbledown, others new, architect-designed, with cars parked outside.

Near the water's edge was a modern hotel and a number of private houses. Each house along the waterfront seemed to possess its own boat or yacht, thus showing what a vital part the fjord played in the lives of the villagers.

Slowly the ship moved towards its mooring and hit the landing stage with a slight jolt. This, said Per's voice over the loudspeakers, was where they were staying for a while, to allow the passengers to leave the ship and explore the village. He told them that if they gathered on the quayside, they would be taken to visit a museum, a folk museum, where they would see many things of interest.

The museum, the visitors discovered, consisted of two wooden buildings and which, even in the bright sunlight, were shadowy and dark. There were few windows and no means of lighting the buildings internally. As Noelle wandered round, she heard Per explaining, in whatever language the questioner happened to speak, the meaning and origin of the objects on display.

In English Per said that the centre of the building had been set out exactly as it used to be in the old days. The 'house', as it would have been to the farming family who had lived in it, was built entirely of timber, and the hole in the roof – Per indicated it – was a form of ventilation and a means of letting out the smoke from the fire.

There were cooking utensils, a spinning wheel, a very old sewing machine. There were ancient farming implements, chairs and furniture. Costumes were on display, too, and there were two full-size figures – a bride and her bridegroom – wearing the traditional Norwegian wedding clothes.

The bridegroom's outfit was black with a green waistcoat

beneath the trimmed jacket. But it was the bridal costume which attracted most attention.

The woman in charge of the museum said, in English, 'It is our custom to request a young lady in the party to wear the bridal clothes for the benefit of her companions. If they wish to take photographs – and people always do – it is so much better if they are modelled outside in the daylight by a real person than by a lifeless figure.'

She looked round the group and her eyes came to rest on Noelle. 'Yes, you will be so good as to model for us? You are so pretty and so slim, I am sure these clothes will fit you.'

Noelle coloured with embarrassment and shook her head. Kirsten, beside her, gave her a slight push. 'Do it, Noelle. Then we can take our pictures and everyone will go away content. Please . . .'

Kirsten was her friend and Noelle, seeing her sweet appealing smile – she had the Arneson charm, there was no doubt about it – felt that she could not refuse. But still she hesitated and looked for guidance from Kirsten's brother.

It seemed he had none to give. His face was impassive, as empty of feeling as an unoccupied house. In fact, Noelle wondered if he had even heard the woman's request. His total indifference nettled her. Why should she not try on the bridal outfit? English she might be, but she was a woman, and the clothes looked so colourful, so inviting they appealed to the designer in her as well as her femininity. Did it matter if she was not Norwegian, if she was not really entitled to wear them?

Noelle nodded at last and there were calls in different languages of 'thank you'. There was no need, the woman said, for Noelle to remove any of her clothes, except her jacket. She was so slim the dress would slip over her head – see? – and button up to the neck. The woman bent down and turned up the hems of Noelle's trousers so that they disappeared beneath the ankle-length skirt.

The waistcoat, scarlet and heavily embroidered, was decorated with gilt 'buttons' of many different sizes and was almost the length of the black skirt underneath it. An embroidered apron fell almost to the hem of the skirt. A white 'bib' was fastened into place and round her neck were placed two gold medallions. A gold belt encircled her waist and on her head was placed a heavy, gold-coloured, jewel-studded crown. Scarlet ribbons, tied under her chin, secured the crown to her head.

The audience was unstinting in its admiration, both of the clothes and of the girl who was wearing them. 'She's so sweet,' whispered one woman. '*Si jolie*,' said another.

When the woman led Noelle outside the crowd followed. Cameras were lifted into position, lenses adjusted, buttons were pressed. It was a long time before the people would let Noelle go. Kirsten had produced a camera from her pocket and seemed to be using up a great deal of film, taking pictures of Noelle from all angles.

'Smile, Noelle,' she called. 'Pretend you're really a bride and that you're going to marry the man you love.' Noelle smiled, suppressing a sudden, traitorous uprush of longing as the face of a man swam into her mind and – as she unconsciously searched for him – into her line of vision. 'Fine,' called Kirsten, 'keep it up!'

No, Per had no camera. He was standing only a short distance away, hands in his pockets, watching her with dark, narrow eyes. There was a hint of sardonic amusement in his expression. Noelle tore her eyes away. What had he read into her look? Whatever it was had made him smile. Perhaps he saw his goal in sight, the goal he avowed he was working towards – her surrender to him, total and absolute.

'Now,' said the woman in charge, standing with her hands clasped in front of her ample figure, 'I will tell you a little about a traditional Norwegian wedding. After the ceremony in the church, there is a procession to the place where the wedding feast is held. First comes the fiddler, then the fathers of the bride and bridegroom, followed by the two respective mothers. Then comes the bride and groom themselves.

'There are musicians who play at the *fest*, the feast, and there is a certain order in which the dances take place. First the bride dances with the master of ceremonies, then with her new father-in-law. After that, she takes her father on to the floor and at last she is allowed to go into the arms of her bridegroom and dance with him. The dancing and eating and drinking go on until midnight or beyond, and it is only then that the happy couple are allowed to depart on their own.'

'A groom,' called an American voice from the crowd, 'give the bride a groom. She looks too cute to be wasted!'

There was laughter, and the American lady called out, looking round,

'Who's going to volunteer?'

'Per,' said Kirsten, who was standing next to him, 'Per, here's your opportunity.'

The firmness with which Per shook his head revealed the strength of his feelings about the matter, but the crowd, having found a tall, fair, handsome Norwegian to fill the vacancy, and the proprietor of the hotel at that, was in no mood to be thwarted.

So they urged him repeatedly to take his place beside the 'bride' and after a few moments Noelle found Per holding her hand and smiling down at her with a taunting glint. 'It seems,' he murmured, 'I have had you wished on me as a wife, which I had no intention of taking. What am I to do with you?'

Noelle looked tremulously up at him. How could she disguise the craving for the fulfilment of the vision which her imagination flashed across her brain, of Per Arneson as her husband? How to keep the desire from her eyes?

'Kiss the bride!' a man called out.

'Yes,' the others took him up, 'kiss her!'

Per looked down at her, eyebrows lifted. 'Well? It seems they're after blood and will not be satisfied until it is spilt.'

His arms came round her and she was swept against him. The kiss was swift, hard and entirely efficient. After all, he knew the geography of her lips by now – he had explored them at least twice before. Cameras clicked. Voices said, 'Hold it, man. One more shot. Don't stop!'

Per's lips lingered and left her limp, the surroundings whirling and the crowd a formless mass. When her mind groped its way out of the mists in which it had been wandering, the faces became identifiable as individual and smiling. Spontaneously, applause broke out, Kirsten's clapping, even if touched with irony, being the loudest of all.

The onlookers, having witnessed the killing, began to disperse. Per, moving to stand in front of Noelle, looked her up and down.

'Having sampled what it would be like to be your husband,' he remarked, 'I'm now in the position to state that one day you will make some man a charming bride. Sadly for all concerned, I shall not be a candidate for the post. But send me a card when you are on your honeymoon.'

CHAPTER SIX

MARK ANDERSON, having apparently given up hope of ever making Noelle his girl-friend, had found another girl with whom to share his walks. Noelle was not sorry. She liked Mark, but had found that, after a while, they had little to talk about.

So, in her spare time and when Kirsten was busy elsewhere, Noelle found herself going alone for walks along the fjord, or climbing a hill and gazing down at the breathtaking view. It was while she was half-way up the hill one afternoon that the clouds began to gather. She buttoned her jacket – she had no covering for her hair, having gone out unprepared for rain – and ran back down the hill, hoping she would make the hotel before the contents of the clouds descended.

As she reached the foot of the hill, the deluge started. A short distance along the fjord and in the opposite direction from the hotel, she saw a hut with a few steps leading up to a covered platform. There was a shout behind her, but she disregarded it. When she reached the shelter of the hut, her hair was flattened with rain which also ran off her jacket and soaked through her sandals to her bare feet. As she parted her hair in order to see, she heard footsteps and stiffened with fright. But the man to whom those footsteps belonged was as familiar to her as a painting hung on a wall, a man whose face appeared constantly in her dreams at night and her thoughts by day. He had been away again for a few days – at another of his hotels, Kirsten had said – yet there he was, back at this hotel, in this village. Hadn't he told her he found there a peace, a contentment, which he could not find elsewhere?

It must have been he who had shouted, and to her, not to someone else. It seemed he had wanted to make his presence known to her. She could not think why. He climbed the steps to the platform and lifted a hand to rake through his rain-soaked hair. He smiled down at her and she wondered just what she must look like. The rain had made no difference to his appearance. His belted jacket had repelled the rain, not absorbed it as hers had done. His hair had not been flattened to his head, instead its thick, honey-gold fairness had been enhanced by the dampness.

With the backs of her hands, Noelle made a frantic attempt to dry her cheeks. A hand went into a trouser pocket and a handkerchief was pulled out of it. 'Any good?' asked Per.

Noelle's hand came out to take it, but Per pushed it aside and stood in front of her, wiping her face gently and tenderly, down her cheeks, over her chin, across her forehead, while she looked up at him like an obedient, unresisting child.

The handkerchief was pushed away and fingers spread out around her throat, tipping up her face. His eyes, seeking, serious, looked into hers and once more Noelle knew the joy of being kissed by him. Her legs grew weak, her body seemed to melt and sway towards him and he put himself against her to steady her.

When he lifted his head, her eyes were moist, not with rain any more but with entreaty. 'Per, please,' she whispered, shaking her head.

'Why not?' There was a smile in the question.

She countered with another question. 'Why do you keep kissing me?'

He threw back his head and laughed. 'Have you looked in the mirror?'

She nodded, feeling his fingers still round her throat. 'I see a perfectly ordinary girl . . . '

'Then your mirror lies. Buy yourself another.'

'You haven't answered my question.'

He looked at her face, every feature, but the smile he gave held a hint of mockery. 'Maybe it's because I like kissing pretty girls, eh?'

Her response came at once. Her hand came up and grasped his wrist, wrenching his hand from her throat. What had she expected? she asked herself bitterly. A declaration that he admired her, desired her beyond all other women? This man, who had known so many.

She moved to the rail around the platform and stared out over the rain-drenched view. 'Why did you come out?' she asked tonelessly.

'Why did *you* come out?'

'Because I felt the urge to – to walk, to get away from everything, everyone for a while.'

'I too felt that same urge. Is it so surprising?'

'And,' stiffly, 'you had to spoil your walk by meeting up with me.'

'That was my fortune or,' with a smile, 'misfortune, whichever way you choose to look at it.'

She tensed but let his baiting pass. The waters of the fjord were dark, mirroring the brooding, mist-veiled mountains. The greens around them – those varied, soothing greens – had darkened. The white of the snow on the summits had dulled under the weight of the rain.

But even as Noelle watched, the sun came from somewhere over the hills and touched the valley, gilding the landscape and lightening the sky.

'Look there.' Per, beside her, was pointing towards a shimmering patch of water. 'If you had brought your camera, you would have been able to "catch" your rainbow. But you have not brought a camera, so your rainbow – alas, like all rainbows – remains elusive and uncaught.'

'Like me,' he should have added, Noelle thought, as she went down the steps and away from him. But he walked beside her in silence, and as they reached the edge of the village, he put out a hand and stopped her, turning her to face him.

'Tell me something, Noelle. You asked me a question back there. Does it upset you when I kiss you? Don't you like my kisses? Do you,' moving a few paces closer, 'want me to stop?'

Her eyes lifted tremulously. How could she answer him? 'I want your kisses, I want *more* than your kisses? I want them to be given not on impulse, at the whim of your desire, but as the result of a much deeper, lasting emotion – love?' What did this man, with his carefully nurtured charm, his attraction for women, the magic wand of his riches, know about love?

'Your kisses?' she whispered, then shook her head. 'I—' She turned and left him standing, running all the way back to the hotel.

It was a rule that every evening there should be two or three girls on duty after the dining-room had closed. They were expected to be available should the guests require service in the form of trays of sandwiches, tea or coffee. Wherever guests happened to be, in the main lounge, the television room or their bedrooms, trays of whatever they required would be taken to them.

That evening it was Noelle's turn to be on duty. Roy Vikör, the assistant *direktör*, came to the kitchens and informed Noelle that Herr Arneson and his guest were in the main lounge. Would she please attend to their requirements? As Noelle straightened her uniform and tidied her hair, she wondered who Per's guest might be. She approached the alcove where Per and his companion were sitting, and thought, I should have known. It was Sonja's free evening and Sonja Linde was Per Arneson's guest.

A feeling which Noelle refused to acknowledge as jealousy tightened her muscles and glazed over her eyes as she stood stiffly beside the couch which the owner and his lady-friend were sharing.

'Well, well,' said Per softly, 'so it's you.' There was a trace of familiarity in his voice which was not accidental. 'I would have thought you would be enjoying your solitude, indulging your desire to "get away from it all" in the sanctuary of your – my – bedroom.' He glanced obliquely at his companion and registered her response with apparent satisfaction.

Sonja rose to the bait – he had so obviously intended to provoke her to jealousy – and asked, her voice rising, '*Your* room? This girl is sleeping in your bedroom?'

Per smiled indolently. He could afford to smile. His lady-friend's response had been so swift, so angry. 'At the staff house, yes. Hasn't the hotel grapevine informed you of that? It's common knowledge amongst the staff.'

Sonja seemed scarcely able to contain her fury. 'So, you two—?'

Per's hand lifted in a soothing motion. 'Don't be so alarmed, my dear. We are,' his eyes laughed up at Noelle's 'how do the English say it, Noelle?' His voice lingered caressingly over her name. 'Just good – very good – friends?'

'Per,' Sonja grasped his arm, 'you cannot do this to me. And for a – for a—' She looked contemptuously at Noelle, seeming lost for words.

'For a mere waitress?' Per supplied, with a broad smile. 'But you're wrong. You see, Noelle is my sister's friend, and therefore entitled to be treated a little – well, differently from the others. Which means that our relationship,' with a goading smile at Noelle, 'is – should be – just a little – er – closer than is usual between boss and, forgive the word,' with a mocking bow to Noelle, 'servant.'

With amusement he watched the colour creep into Noelle's cheeks. 'Your order, Herr Arneson?'

But it was Sonja who gave the order. 'We wish for coffee and two open sandwiches.'

'Which,' Per added, 'in Norwegian we call *en snitte platte* – a plate of open sandwiches. You have heard Olaf Krüger speak of them?'

Noelle nodded, wishing he would not be so informal with her when she was on duty. Unless there was a purpose behind his friendly manner. Hearing the sharpness of Sonja's tone, Noelle guessed he was intent on increasing her jealousy.

Sonja waved her away. 'The chef will know what I like – a little tongue, a little salami, perhaps some salmon or egg.'

But in the kitchens the chef was not on duty. His assistant was there and when Noelle passed Sonja's order on, he shrugged. 'She is the boss's woman, so she thinks she can behave like the great lady,' he muttered. 'She will have what I give her and like it!'

But Sonja did not like it. They were not what she had ordered, she said. The chef knew perfectly well she could not stand that particular type of cold meat. She became abusive towards Noelle as if she had prepared the food herself. Noelle looked at Per, expecting his support, but he was lounging against the cushioned back of the alcove, watching the flaring of her anger against Sonja's unjust accusation. But he did nothing to stem the flow of his lady-friend's abuse.

Noelle, resenting strongly the injustice that was being meted out to her, could not contain that anger. 'If you'll please be quiet for one moment, Fröken Linde, and allow me to speak . . .'

Sonja was so surprised at Noelle's tone she stopped in mid-sentence.

'Miss Roberts!' Per's voice held a warning which she disregarded. She was not going to let 'the boss's woman' walk verbally all over her. Even if Per objected, she intended to defend herself against his girl-friend's undeserved censure.

'I did not make your sandwiches, Fröken Linde,' Noelle said quietly, 'so it's hardly fair to blame me if the food is not to your liking. The chef didn't make them, either.'

'Then, Miss Roberts,' Noelle looked at Per as he addressed her, and his displeasure with her was unmistakable, 'who did prepare the sandwiches?'

'The assistant chef, Herr Arneson.'

'Take them back,' Sonja said imperiously. 'I have lost my appetite. Per, this girl has been insolent towards me again.

How can you sit there and let her get away with it? She's not fit to be a waitress. You should make her apologize as you did once before.'

Per sighed. 'Apologize, Miss Roberts.'

Noelle shot him a look so full of resentment he must have felt its impact. 'I don't consider, Fröken Linde, that I have been insolent. I was merely stating facts. I—'

'*Apologize*, Miss Roberts,' the long-suffering note had been replaced by curtness, 'or I shall fire you on the spot!'

'All right, Herr Arneson, fire me!' Her lip quivered as she spoke. 'I'm not going to apologize for something I haven't done.'

As she walked with dignity towards the swing doors leading to the kitchens, she knew it was the end. She had gone too far this time. It was not quite the end of her time on duty, but it was no use staying now. She could not face another customer. The head waiter understandingly agreed to allow her to go off duty a little early because of a 'headache'.

Instead of returning to her room, Noelle crossed the entrance foyer of the hotel and ran along the corridor leading to Per's apartment. He would not be there because he was in the lounge, and not even Per Arneson could be in two places at once. But, she hoped, Kirsten would be there.

Noelle knocked, glancing round anxiously to make sure Per had not followed and, hearing Kirsten's invitation, went in. As soon as Kirsten saw Noelle's face, she became concerned.

'Something's wrong. What's happened?'

Noelle shook her head, unable to speak, and burst into tears. Kirsten drew her into the room and closed the door.

'Now tell me all about it,' Kirsten invited, and Noelle did, sinking on to the floor beside the dress Kirsten had been cutting out.

Through clenched teeth Kirsten said, 'Every time I talk about – *think* about – that woman of his, I want to lift my hands and do this!' She curled her fingers and pretended to fit them round her neck. 'How can he take her part—'

The door opened and Per came in. Kirsten said indignantly, 'I think you should apologize to Noelle.'

Per ignored his sister. Noelle did not lift her head from her hands and he spoke to her bent head. 'I went to the kitchens. You were not there. I went to your – my – room. You were not there either. I might have known you would come complaining to my sister.'

'Leave her alone,' Kirsten stormed. 'She's my friend, my best friend. I brought her over here. Haven't you done enough damage? Firing her like that, while she was on duty, and all because of that – that bitch of a woman, that *kvinnfolk* you run around with.'

He turned on his sister, '*Vær stille!* Be silent! Keep out of this. I'm in charge of this hotel, not you. In any case, I have not fired your precious friend, your *beste venninne*.' Turning to Noelle, 'I have not even fired my employee.'

'You have,' Noelle responded accusingly. 'If I didn't apologize, you said, you'd fire me on the spot. I refused to apologize, so that's that, isn't it?'

'You want to leave?'

Noelle stared, puzzled by the question. If she said 'no', she would put it into his power to dismiss her and then delight in her humiliation. So she took refuge in a spate of reproach. 'You insulted me, you tried to make me apologize for something I just didn't do. It happened that time Miss Linde jogged my arm as I was serving the soup. You didn't believe me when I told you the truth, and you made me apologize when it was not my fault. She was being quite impossible this evening, abusing me, blaming me ... And instead of taking my part, you turned on me, too.'

'Will you be quiet, Miss Roberts?' Anger added a dangerous light to his eyes. A little more, Noelle thought dully, and he would be marching her from the room and throwing her out of the door.

'You may be my sister's friend, but you came here to work for me for your own benefit, not mine.' He looked her over.

'I seem to recall that I had grave doubts as to your suitability for the job right from the start.'

'It's hardly fair to judge me on this incident.'

'Not only this incident. The other, too, which also involved Miss Linde.'

'All right,' Noelle conceded sulkily, 'on those two incidents alone. No other guest has treated me as insultingly as Miss Linde.'

'Then you've been lucky, Miss Roberts.'

'Anyway,' Noelle, although acknowledging that he was trying to be reasonable, was determined to be her own advocate, 'Miss Linde is a member of staff, as I am.'

'But she was off duty. The fact that she's a member of staff does not enter into it. At the times we are talking of, she was a guest – my guest, and as such, demanded and should have been accorded the respect and attention given to all the guests who patronize my hotels. I might add that if any other waitress had spoken about a guest in her presence as you did – no matter who that guest was – I would have been greatly tempted to put her bodily out of the hotel lounge, out of the building and out of her job!'

Noelle's head drooped and she played with a box of pins which were on the carpet beside Kirsten's dress. 'Miss Linde was being obnoxious,' she murmured, her indignation crumbling as something inside her admitted he was right.

Kirsten muttered her agreement, but her brother snapped, 'I told you, keep out of this.' Then, 'Obnoxious is a strong word, Miss Roberts.' Again the warning in his voice. 'But there are many guests who are obnoxious, as you put it, who are insulting and quite, quite impossible. But whatever they might be, however offensively they might behave towards the staff, *they are guests*, and have to be treated with courtesy and respect, however furious you may be feeling inside. Look at me, Miss Roberts.' Slowly Noelle raised her head and her tear-dulled eyes looked into his. For a moment, he looked back at her and for a passing second something – was it compassion? – flickered in his gaze. 'Do you understand what I'm saying?'

The hint of a softening in his manner had her heart pounding. She looked at his lips, less taut now as his anger died away, and remembered the feel of them on hers.

'I'm sorry,' she muttered, rising to her feet. 'It won't happen again, because I shall be leaving tomorrow. There's no need to pay my salary for this week. I'll forfeit it—'

'I asked you a question earlier,' Per said stiffly. 'You did not answer it. Do you want to leave?'

This time she had no option but to reply, but she could not put it into words. She shook her head.

'You want to stay?'

'I want to stay,' she whispered.

'As Kirsten's friend?' She looked at him, surprised. 'As a guest of the family? Or remaining as a member of my staff?'

As a guest of the family? At his expense, because that was what it would be. She could not put herself into his debt like that, but Kirsten urged,

'Stay on, Noelle, make the rest of your time here a holiday. We can put up another bed in my room.'

But Noelle shook her head. 'I couldn't take advantage of your brother's generosity.' Kirsten began to remonstrate, but Noelle said to Per, 'As your employee – if you'll allow me to.'

She was, she knew, humbling herself, that she was putting herself entirely at his mercy. If he wanted to let the axe fall, severing all her connections with him here and now, he had it in his power to do so.

He was so long in answering, Noelle began to despair. She wandered across to the window and idly picked up a miniature troll which stood on the sill. Absently she stroked its long, soft hair and gazed into the pixie-like face. Still Per had not spoken. Kirsten went into her bedroom and the sound of an electric sewing maching came out of it.

This, Noelle supposed, staring out at the fjord rippling in the moonlight, was the end of her journey. She lifted the troll and stared at it as if in its strange features, its enigmatic half-smile, she might find the answer Per seemed unable to give. A hand took the troll from her and she turned, startled. Per had moved so quietly she had not heard him.

He looked at the troll. 'You like him? He was given to me as a child. I cherished him for years. There is a tale told about a troll. Not so far from here is a rock fashioned into a troll's giant foot. Trolls come in all sizes, you know.' His smile was gently mocking. 'This troll,' his smile grew warmer, speeding Noelle's heartbeats, '– he was old, of course – was sitting on a rock one day, thinking – well, about things in general. Now a troll, you know,' again that smile, this time with a twinkle, 'must never be caught in the sunlight, but he was so engrosssed in his thoughts, he failed to notice that the sun had come out.

'When he saw the sun, he was so horrified he vanished quickly into the underground tunnel where he lived – all trolls live underground, you see – but he was not quite quick enough. The sun just caught his foot. It was turned at once into stone, and there it is to this day, in the rock. You like that tale?' She nodded, smiling back at him, feeling the depression inside her lighten. 'It is legendary. I heard it when I was a child. Every time I looked at my troll, I always felt glad he had not been caught in the sunlight and that he had two feet.' Per held the troll out to her. 'You would like my troll?'

She put her hands behind her, horrified. 'Take something from your childhood, something you loved so much?'

'I'm offering him to you. Would you like him? He will bring you luck, as he brought me.' He lifted her hand, opened it and placed the troll in her palm, closing her fingers over it. His hand felt warm against hers.

'Is it,' she had to know, 'is it a farewell gift?'

'Farewell? Why, are you leaving?' His eyes were ingenuous, his eyebrows high.

He was not sending her away! Dumb with joy, she shook

her head. 'Thank you for – for giving me another chance,' she whispered. 'I'll try not to let you down again.'

The ice, she thought abstractedly, the ice she used to see in those eyes – she must have imagined it.

His hand tilted her face. '*Min kjære* Noelle,' he whispered, 'my sweet girl, let me down?'

As his lips lowered towards hers, Kirsten came into the lounge, stopped, said, 'Oh, dear, am I interrupting something?' and disappeared again.

But the moment had passed. Per went out, leaving Noelle staring out of the windows, her lips untouched.

Kirsten, hearing the door close, came back. 'Sorry I broke up the love scene.' Her tone was sarcastic. 'What was my brother doing, using his charm to soothe you, calm you down?'

Noelle hid the troll. For some reason, she did not want Kirsten to know that Per had given it to her. Somehow Kirsten, with her acid comments, would desecrate Per's unselfish gesture in giving her the long-cherished, tiny figure.

'I suppose,' replied Noelle a little sadly, 'you could say that.'

Kirsten gave a short laugh. 'Yes, he would. He turns on the charm whenever he thinks it will benefit him most. And always it's a woman at the receiving end. The more attractive that woman,' she went on with asperity, 'the greater the dose of charm. If he wanted a woman enough he would even tell her he loved her if it would make her say "yes" and give him what he wanted.'

Noelle asked faintly, wondering how Kirsten knew so much about her brother's private life, 'And does he often – "want" a woman? I thought the women ran after him.'

'They do, nauseatingly frequently. But now and then one of them can be a little difficult and he makes the running.' She shrugged and laughed. 'I suppose life becomes a bit more interesting for him if he has to chase instead of stand still and let them come to him.'

Kirsten returned to the bedroom. Noelle brought the troll from behind her back, seeking, by studying it and remembering the strange generosity of Per's gift of it, to assuage the pain Kirsten's words had inflicted. As she stared into the troll's curiously bright eyes, she tried vainly to unravel the secrets they held. Then she lifted it and pressed it to her cheek.

CHAPTER SEVEN

BREAKFASTS were over and the staff were free to go to their coffee break. Noelle noticed, as she crossed the entrance foyer on her way to the staff house, that Per was in his office behind the reception desk.

A young man was lounging against the desk. Beside him on the floor was a bulging rucksack. He wore a grey parka lined in scarlet and his hair was so fair it was almost white.

He turned and saw Noelle. Recognition had his eyes, his mouth and his arms open all at once. 'Hey, little girl! I have found you again, and so soon! I am just booking in to the hotel and there you are, almost as if you had known I was coming.' He came towards her and she was enveloped in a bear hug.

Other guests smiled indulgently as he kissed her cheek. 'I am Einar Olsen. You remember me? We met on the ship coming across the North Sea. You could not surely have forgotten so soon?' He held her away. 'I have come this long journey to see you again. You see, I have not forgotten *you.*'

'Miss Roberts!' Noelle jerked out of Einar's arms to face her employer. His mouth was tight, his eyes narrow. The ice was back. 'This is the foyer of the hotel. You may be off duty for ten minutes, but you are still in uniform.'

He stopped. He did not need to say any more, because the warning was there. Noelle stared back at him reproachfully. He was putting her in the wrong again, as if she were responsible for the situation. How could she help it if Einar was so pleased to see her he wanted the world to know? But her eyes fell before Per's. After last night's bitter quarrel and last night's truce, she did not want to annoy him again.

What had she promised? 'I'll try not to let you down.'

'I'm sorry, Herr Arneson.' To Einar, 'I'll be free after lunches have been served. If you like, you can see me then.'

He looked at Per and then at Noelle. He made such a wry face Noelle laughed. Per made an angry movement.

'Where shall I see you?' Einar asked.

'Outside the staff house across the road,' Noelle said.

'Never fear, I will be waiting,' Einar told her.

Per slammed his door.

That afternoon the sun was warm. The pool seemed hardly big enough to accommodate all the guests who were splashing and diving and swimming in it. Einar had persuaded Noelle to join him there.

They had swum and now they were sunbathing. Noelle was towelling her legs and Einar was lying beside her. They were on the far side of the pool with their backs to the fjord and facing the hotel. Noelle's eyes were drawn towards Per's apartment. The door leading on to the paved walk was open.

Per stood outside, leaning shoulders to the wall, watching them. His shirt was unbuttoned and flapping loosely in the breeze. His hands were in the pockets of his trousers which were, although casual, well-tailored and snug-fitting over his hips and thighs. He looked indolently handsome and Noelle's pulses hammered. There was no escaping the fact – the mere sight of him excited her, and despite the cynicism which tightened the smile playing over his mouth, she could not tear her eyes away.

So she was behaving like all his other women. As he looked back at her, could he see implicit in her glance the 'open arms' he talked of so disparagingly, the arms he invariably ran towards?

What was the use of being attracted to him? she asked herself despairingly. Where would it lead, except to heartbreak and years of misery? Because it would take years to forget such a man as Per Arneson, if ever one got too emotionally involved with him. Had she reached that stage now? Was it already too late? That was something she would not admit, even to herself. The possibility both sickened and frightened her.

'Hey, Noelle, your eyes are sad. You are dreaming unhappy dreams.' Einar pulled her down beside him and rolled over to look at her, face down. 'I've come all the way from my aunt's house in Bergen just to see you. Concentrate on me, *elskling* – how you say in English? – darling. I want to kiss you, little kitten, and you cannot stop me.'

Noelle could certainly not stop him. He did not even give her time to try. His kiss was long-lasting and as thoroughly extrovert as he was himself. When he had finished, he made loud appreciative noises and the guests around them laughed. With a struggle Noelle sat up. She looked anxiously for Per and caught the end of a contemptuous glance he had flung at her. Then he went into his apartment, securing the door so carefully and precisely the action was almost an insult in itself.

Einar asked Noelle to dine with him that evening.

'I can't,' she told him, 'I have to serve dinner myself.'

'Tomorrow, then,' he persisted. 'Surely you have an evening off sometimes?'

'Tomorrow I'm free. Are you sure, Einar? Are you sure you have enough—'

'Money?' he broke in. 'But of course.' He made the action of emptying non-existent pockets in his swimming briefs. 'I have hundreds and hundreds of *kroner*. Haven't I just visited my dear aunt, and is she not so fond of me she would give me her entire fortune if I asked?'

Noelle laughed. 'Is she rich?'

'Well,' he smiled, playing with her hair, 'not really. But she did give me money. Enough to have a few days' holiday, enough to take a girl out. So will you dine with me, kitten?' She nodded. 'It will be good, will it not, being unpleasant to your colleagues, while you sit like a lady at the table?'

Noelle laughed and detached her hair from his fingers, but he grabbed it and with it pulled her down beside him so that she could not get away. Then he kissed her again.

'Stop it, Einar!' she protested, wishing he were not so uninhibited in the display of his desires and so unrestrained in the indulgence of them. She struggled free and stood up.

Einar whistled. 'You have no conception of how beautiful you are in that swimsuit, Noelle.' His hands fashioned feminine curves.

'You exaggerate terribly. I don't believe you.'

'Look around. Look at all the men looking at you. You see what is in their eyes? Longing, Noelle, desire. Which is what I am feeling for you.' He dived for her legs, but she evaded him, pulling on her wrap and seeking with a kind of fear for the figure at the window.

Yes, Per was there, staring out. He was too far away for her to see his expression, but she could guess what it would be. Contempt, as it was before, derision, even disgust?

For dinner that evening Einar put himself at one of Noelle's tables. He joked with her, keeping her waiting for his order while the other guests grew restive. Per sat at his own table, but still Einar kept her. It was as though he was doing it to provoke Per's anger, knowing that because he was a guest, Per Arneson was powerless to stop him.

In the end, Noelle walked away, but even so, Einar called after her. She ignored him, going straight to Per's table, the pencil in her hand trembling a little.

Per raised his head and shock went through her. The ice was there again. His eyes were colder than they had ever been. If she apologized, would he forgive her? But he gave her no chance. 'Attend to the other guests,' he said quietly. 'They have been waiting longer than I.'

She did as he directed, but the other guests had waited so long they were petulant and difficult about their orders. Noelle kept glancing at Per, trying to tell him with her eyes how sorry she was, but he would not look at her. In the end, he pushed back his chair and left the dining-room, and there came a long, loud sigh from Einar's table.

Dinner dragged on, but Per did not return. Noelle supposed that he had had his meal served in his flat. What would he say to her now? But couldn't he see it was not her fault? That is was Einar who was the cause of the trouble?

At last her tables were empty and she cleared them, carrying the tray into the kitchen. The door swung open behind her. 'Hey, little girl, I could have carried that. I called to you. Did you not hear me?'

'Einar!' Noelle whispered hoarsely.

He grinned. 'I am your friend, so I follow you around.'

'Fröken Roberts!' Noelle turned to find the head waiter glaring at her. 'What is this man doing here? Boy-friends are not allowed in the kitchens. Tell him, go, please. At once.' The staff around them stopped working to watch.

'He's – he's not my boy-friend, Herr Krüger. He's a guest.'

'Tell him to go!' Herr Krüger shouted. 'At once, please.'

'Einar, you'll get me into terrible trouble.'

Einar folded his arms. 'If you will kiss me, I will go.'

Olaf Krüger made an explosive sound and marched out of the kitchens.

One of the girls spoke to Einar in Norwegian and he laughed loudly. 'There, Noelle, she says if you won't kiss me, she will. Now, do you want me to stay, or—?'

Noelle reached up and kissed him on the cheek. 'Now go, Einar.'

Einar said, 'That was not what I meant, but it will do. For now.'

As Einar left, Olaf Krüger came back. 'Fröken Roberts, you are to see Herr Arneson in his office.'

No, Noelle thought, her heart sinking, not again! Not another argument, another quarrel.

'I hear,' Per greeted her coldly, 'that you have been causing trouble again. And you have been insolent to the *hov-*

mester, Herr Krüger.'

'Insolent to Herr Krüger? How can he say that?'

'He tells me that when he ordered you to send your boy-friend from the kitchens, you did not do so. Instead, you tried to make excuses.'

'It's not true, Herr Arneson. I told Herr Krüger that Einar was not my boy-friend, he was a guest. And, as you have so often told me, Herr Arneson,' her eyes rested ingenuously on his, 'guests in your hotels are sacrosanct, and to be pampered, their slightest whim indulged. So if a guest of yours wanted to visit the kitchens, how could I tell him to go?'

Per's lips thinned, his fingers twitched. 'If I had my way, I would put you across my knee.'

'But, Herr Arneson, I'm speaking the truth. It's something you have told me continuously since I started to work for you. Guests are—'

He walked towards her. 'Don't try me too far! Just because you're my sister's friend, it doesn't mean you can get away with murder – or its verbal equivalent.'

Her eyes quivered before the cold anger in his. 'I'm sorry, Herr Arneson.' It was such familiar phrase, too familiar, she thought. 'I – I don't ever mean to take advantage of my friendship with Kirsten. If it seems like that I can only repeat that I'm sorry.'

There was a long silence. At the end of it, Noelle knew the pattern on the carpet by heart. 'Tell me,' Per said, 'has my *guest* left the kitchen now?' Noelle nodded. 'How did you persuade him to – shall we say – end his tour of inspection?'

She murmured in reply, 'He – he insisted that I kissed him.' She lifted her eyes and found that he was smiling. 'May I go?' she whispered.

'Yes, and quickly, before I demand of you what your boy-friend demanded in payment for allowing you to go!'

Noelle turned and fled.

Kirsten said in Per's apartment the following afternoon, 'Who's the new boy-friend?'

Noelle explained how she had met him on the ship. 'He comes from North Cape. Nordkapp, he called it.'

'And,' said Kirsten, 'you can't get much farther north in this country than that! So you met him coming over on the ferry. Why didn't you tell me he was coming here?'

'I didn't know myself. I'd almost forgotten him. He's rather sweet, but – well, a nuisance at times. He's invited me to dine with him tonight.'

Kirsten laughed loudly. 'I shall join Per for dinner, too. I must see his face when you come into the dining-room – as a guest!'

'Don't tell him,' Noelle pleaded.

'Why,' Kirsten asked, amused, 'do you think he will turn you away at the door?'

But Per was not in the dining-room when Noelle and Einar took their places at a table for two. He came in with Kirsten when Noelle's head was close to Einar's, reading the menu.

Kirsten put her arm round Noelle's shoulders and hugged her, then she moved round to speak to Einar. They conversed in Norwegian and Noelle heard the word Nordkapp, Einar's home town.

Per stood beside Noelle, looking down at her. There was no mistaking the amusement he was feeling. He said, falsely solicitous, 'Is everything to your liking, Miss Roberts? Is the service good enough? Are your wants being attended to by the staff, your every wish granted, your every whim indulged?'

He was, of course, laughing at her and throwing her own words back, playing the over-attentive proprietor, probably to embarrass her. But she was not embarrassed. She smiled up at him, asking softly,

'What are you now, Herr Arneson? Kirsten's brother or my employer?'

'Neither, *min kjære* Miss Roberts. You are at this

moment my guest, and I am your host, assiduous for your comfort, concerned for your pleasure.' With a mocking smile, 'Don't hesitate to report to me if the slightest thing is wrong or,' the smile broadened, 'if by any chance you happen to get a waitress who is rebellious, gauche in the way she serves you, answers you back and refuses to apologize when she is in the wrong!'

With a low, derisive bow he moved to his own table. Kirsten, with a lift of the hand, followed.

Einar commented, 'Some girl, that. The boss's sister?'

Noelle nodded. 'The men cluster around her like hungry birds round a crust of bread.'

Einar laughed. 'I like that, *elskling*! You do not mind if I call you "darling" in my own language? You do not object to such familiarity? You see, we Norwegians are rather a reserved people. We keep our endearments – not that we have many – for our immediate family or intimate acquaintances.'

'But,' Noelle picked up the menu and flicked through it, 'I'm not one of your – intimate acquaintances.'

'Yes, well . . .' he took the menu from her with a cheeky grin and fanned himself with it, 'not yet, perhaps. But there is time, is there not, in which a lot of things can happen?'

Maria came to stand at their table. She recognized Noelle and smiled broadly. She looked at Einar and turned her eyes to the ceiling, then bent down and whispered, 'You will be late in bed yourself now, eh? You will not be so—' she made a face – 'so forbidding towards other girls who have loving boy-friends?'

'Is that what she is like?' Einar asked Maria. 'Forbidding? Ah, I will change that soon.' And Maria laughed, checking herself immediately with a hand over her mouth and glancing guiltily at Per. 'I must behave,' she whispered, 'or I will get the telling off like you are always having.'

Over dinner, Einar told her about his home in the far north of Norway, within the Arctic Circle. 'I have some photographs which I must show you in my room. It was named the North Cape by one of your countrymen, Richard Chancellor, in 1553. In midsummer there is no night and in midwinter no day. In the winter months, people start work earlier in the day, finishing early so that they can go skiing. Everyone skis in Norway. It is our national sport.

'For two months in midwinter, there is complete darkness. At around noon,' he told her, 'there is a soft haze with the trees and houses appearing like shadows. But all the houses are brightly lit because electricity is cheap from our hydro-electric power.'

'The Midnight Sun?' Noelle prompted. 'It's something I should love to see.'

'It is worth seeing. Where I live, the whole disc of the Midnight Sun is visible from mid-May until the end of July. We have two months of complete daylight in the summer and the world at night is enveloped in a golden glow.'

'How do you get to sleep?' Noelle asked.

Einar shrugged. 'You do not seem to need so much sleep in the summer night hours. We visit each other whatever the time. It's nothing unusual for someone to call on you at midnight! Young people make a fire and sit round it and sing to their guitars. One day you must visit us in Nordkapp. We would give you a good welcome.'

Noelle touched his hand. 'You're very kind, Einar, but it would hardly be fair. I don't really know you, do I?'

He switched their hands about and covered hers. Nervously, Noelle glanced at Per. Yes, he was watching. She could not read the expression on his face, and its very blankness worried her.

'We could get to know each other,' Einar said. 'After all, why else am I here?'

'But you told me you have a girl-friend in England, a girl-friend here in Norway—'

'A man can change, can't he?' Einar responded, pretending to be hurt. 'You would not marry me off to someone I didn't want?'

Noelle laughed and gave up. Afterwards they danced in the cellar. They drank and danced alternately, Einar drinking more than Noelle. In the semi-darkness, Einar kissed her two or three times. Noelle did not repel him because they were gentle kisses and meant nothing.

So it was with a shock that she realized there was a man lurking in the shadows – there were so many shadows in that cellar – and he was leaning back in his alcove seat, legs crossed, hand wrapped around a glass which rested on the table. And once again he was watching them.

The music was strident, the coloured lights moved over the dancers. Sonja, who was behind the bar in a corner, laughed loudly, the grating quality it contained competing with the music.

Noelle remembered the last time she had come to the cellar. Per had danced with her and kissed her, too, but what a different response he had evoked in her. As they passed near him, he did not smile. There was a brooding look on his face and a cynical evaluation in his drooping eyelids. It told Noelle exactly what he was thinking. Let him think! she told herself defiantly, forcing herself to yield to Einar's persuasive arms or, when the beat became faster, match her movements to the twisting sensuality of his.

If her apparent submission to Einar's undoubted physical attractions made Per Arneson realize that there was at least one woman in the world who could resist his own accomplished charm, then she would persist in her provocative response to Einar's encouragement.

Towards the end of the evening, Einar led her from the cellar. He would, he said, like to show her those photographs of his home town. They were in his rucksack in the hotel bedroom. Would she come?

Einar made his invitation sound so normal, the pleasure he anticipated in showing her the pictures so genuine. Noelle did not hesitate in her acceptance. They sat on the bed and Einar passed the photographs across to her. Some of them were shots of the Midnight Sun.

'That's me, fishing at midnight,' he said. 'My sister took it.' In the distance was another man in a rowing boat. 'My father,' Einar said.

In another picture the yellow sun shone out of a bronze sky, its reflection streaming like molten gold across the water. In the foreground was a great rock, the side nearest to the camera being in semi-darkness.

'Me, again,' Einar pointed to a figure sitting on the shores of a fjord, gazing at the yellow disc sinking towards the horizon but which would not set that night or for many nights afterwards.

'To go on a boat trip while the Midnight Sun is up there,' he indicated the sky of another photograph, 'is unforgettable. All round you the water is a kind of red gold. The sky has clouds in it which reflect the rays as if they were lined with gold, yet the mountains are black and in shadow.'

Picture after picture showed Noelle just how beautiful Norway's north country was, and she became determined that one day she would visit it.

Einar put away the photographs and came to sit beside her again. He took her hands. 'Do you have to go, Noelle? Won't you stay?' His eyes pleaded. 'Please. You are so sweet,' he stroked her hair, 'like a soft little kitten.'

She stood to evade his hand. 'I'm sorry, Einar. I must go. It's been a lovely evening. And,' she edged towards the door, 'the dinner. Thank you for it all.'

His mouth turned down. 'Is this all the thanks I get?' He came across and put his hands on her shoulders. 'Nothing more? Not even a kiss?'

'Of course, you can kiss me if you like.'

'So – how you say? – lukewarm, she is! If I like, she says! I do *love* to kiss you.' And he did, but this time it was not gentle and after a few moments Noelle twisted away from him. Her face was flushed.

'Good night, Einar,' She opened the door. 'And thank you for everything.' She went out, thankful that he had not come after her. But she was not alone in the corridor. Sonja approached, a twisted smile on her face. 'So you have on your list two men now? Per will be so interested.' She stopped. 'You have enjoyed your – ' she looked at Einar's door, 'fun? You look as if you have. Good night, Miss Roberts. Happy dreams!'

When, the following evening, Einar heard that Noelle was on duty, he moaned. 'I will follow you around,' he said. 'Wherever you go, I will come.'

'But, Einar, the last time you did that, I was nearly dismissed. If I get into any more trouble, it will be the last.'

'All right,' he conceded, 'I won't follow you with my feet – only with my eyes!' He laughed loudly. 'Why do you look so shocked? You are so worth looking at I won't be bored. I can gaze at your – figure and exercise my imagination.'

Einar sat in the lounge and each time Noelle was called there for service, he kept his promise – he did not take his eyes off her. Whenever she passed him – and he had placed himself in such a position that she had to – he would whisper her name, bringing an embarrassed flush to her cheeks. If other guests saw him and complained . . .

She was told by the head waiter to take a tray of crispbread and coffee to Herr Arneson's office. When she knocked and entered, her heart pounding, Per looked up. He seemed surprised to see her, but there was no pleasure, no welcome for her. He nodded coldly and indicated that she should put the tray on the desk. Then his eyes sought his work again. She might have been a stranger instead of a friend of his sister's, instead of a girl he had held in his arms and kissed. Had Sonja told him about meeting her as she left Einar's room? As she closed the office door, Noelle realized Per had not even thanked her.

Einar had gone by the time she returned to the lounge. She was not sorry, in fact she went limp with relief. But when she was directed by Olaf Krüger to take a tray of coffee and biscuits to room sixteen, she wondered why Einar had not stayed in the lounge to give his order. It was not like Einar to prefer the solitude of his room to the company of others.

Noelle tapped at his door. He opened it with a sweeping bow and she carried the tray in, putting it on the bedside table. He closed the door and stood with his back to it.

'Ah,' he said, rubbing his hands, 'it is so good to be waited on by a beautiful waitress. All the evening I have feasted my eyes. Now I feast my appetite.'

He approached her, arms extended. 'Come, little girl, you will kiss me? Just one as an appetizer before I drink my coffee?' His fingers were loosely round her arms, but as she tried to twist away, they tightened.

'Don't be silly, Einar,' she said sharply. 'I'm on duty. I can't stay here.' She forced a smile. 'You're determined to make me lose my job, aren't you?'

'You are on duty and you are doing your duty. I am a guest, remember?'

He let her go and crossed to the tray to pour some coffee. He lifted the cup, toasting her. 'To our continued friendship. May we get closer than we have ever been.' He put the cup to his lips and drank. 'Now you, Noelle. Drink to us.'

To humour him Noelle put her lips to the other side of the cup, then she went to the door. The handle moved but the door did not open.

'Einar, you've locked it!' Her hand came out for the key. 'Stop fooling, I must get back to the kitchens. I don't know what Herr Krüger will say. We're terribly busy this evening.'

But Einar just looked at her, tipping back his head and finishing the coffee. 'Einar,' her voice lifted uncertainly, 'the key, *please*!'

Slowly he shook his head. 'I have you, I keep you, for as long as I want. Last night you escaped from me. Tomorrow I must go home. Tonight is all we have left, so tonight I keep you here.'

Noelle began to panic. 'You can't, against my will. I'll

bang on the door. I'll shout—'

It was accomplished in a second. Noelle found herself on the bed being forced back against the pillows. Her feet were lifted up and Einar was beside her, pinning her down.

She struggled and twisted, tangling up the bedclothes. 'Einar,' she cried, 'you've gone mad! You've—'

His mouth, bearing down, cut off her protests.

There was a knocking on the door. A voice called, a too-familiar, angry voice. 'Miss Roberts, are you there? Open this door, please. Herr Olsen, I wish to speak with you.'

Einar rolled off the bed, grinning at Noelle. 'Your master calls. You must obey. He's the one, isn't he, he's the one you love? I can tell from your face.'

The truth from his lips hit her forcibly, took the breath – all that he had left her with – from her lungs. 'No, it's not true—'

Before she had time to struggle upright, the door had been unlocked and Per was in the room, staring down at her. Disgust, contempt, even hate was in his eyes. His anger was glacier-cold and Noelle thought, if only he would rage at me, shout at me, show some emotion . . .

He said, 'Out, Miss Roberts,' moving his head towards the door. She stood unsteadily, her legs reluctant to function, but she obeyed. To Einar he said frigidly, 'Please excuse me, Herr Olsen, for the interruption.'

Einar shrugged, smiled and reached for a biscuit. 'We can continue later. She cannot surely be on duty all night. She can return as soon as she is free. I shall be waiting, Noelle.'

'Einar!' The cry was anguished, the tone unbelieving that he could implicate her so deeply, when it was his fault and his alone.

The door closed. 'Miss Roberts!' Slowly she turned to face Per. 'You will collect your belongings and go.'

The colour drained from her face. 'You're turning me out?' She looked wildly up and down the corridor. It was useless to declare her innocence. She had done so many times. He had not believed her before, why should he believe her now? 'It's dark, it's night-time. Where will I go?'

He was unmoved by her plea. He strode away along the corridor and she ran after him. She was forced to defend herself after all. 'I took Einar coffee, Herr Arneson. He locked the door. I couldn't get out.'

But even as she spoke, she realized how feeble it sounded. Finding her as he had done, on the bed, crumpled, dishevelled – what man, having seen her like that, would think differently from the way Per was thinking?

He stood still at last and said, as though she had not spoken, 'I heard from Sonja that you were in Einar Olsen's room last night, but what you do in your free time is your concern. What you do when you are on duty is very much my concern. I've given you chance after chance. This time you have gone too far. You went into a guest's room in the course of your work and stayed there, which is forbidden. It was obvious you had settled down for the night, so don't try to pretend to me that you were an unwilling partner.' His eyes were ice, burning her skin. 'You will go at once.'

He moved forward, but she ran in front of him. 'Please,' she pleaded, and her fingers curled round his arm, shaking it a little as if trying to shake some compassion into him, '*please*, Herr Arneson, let me stay. It wasn't my fault, it wasn't . . .'

He gripped her wrist, dislodging her hand and throwing it aside. He moved through the doors, letting them swing back regardless of whether or not they hit her.

The desire to cry was so strong it took away her breath. She had to use all the self-control she possessed to hold back the sobs that tore at her throat. She made her way to the kitchens. It was important that the head waiter be told that she was no longer a member of the hotel staff.

But as she pushed her way into the kitchens the sobs she had held back had their way and racked her body. A chair stood near a table and she collapsed into it. People crowded round and Mark Anderson put his arms round her shoulders, but Herr Krüger ordered everybody away.

'What has happened, Fröken Roberts? Are you ill?'

She shook her head. 'I – I've been fired,' she sobbed.

'You mean you have been dismissed? On whose orders?'

'Herr Arneson's. I was in Einar Olsen's room – he k-kept me there. I c-couldn't help it—'

'But you *cannot* be dismissed. I am now two short already. Maria and Sophia have quit. They have gone to join the staff of their boy-friends' hotel in the village. I cannot lose you, Fröken Roberts. Herr Arneson – I shall have to speak with Herr Arneson.'

'It's no use,' Noelle whispered, 'he won't change his mind.'

But Per Arneson sent for her. Wearily she dragged herself to his office. The tears were damp on her cheeks and he looked her over coldly, totally unmoved by her misery.

'It seems,' he said, 'you must stay on after all. Much against my will I have had to revoke my dismissal of you and have had to accept you on to my staff again. But I am warning you – one more transgression and you are out – out, do you understand? *For good!*' His fist hammered on the desk.

Noelle made no response but turned and went to the door. With her hand on the handle, she said quietly, her voice wavering, 'Thank you for keeping me on.'

She gazed at him, hoping for some softening, but his face was implacable. She went out.

Einar left next morning. Noelle did not see him again, but he left a note with one of the other waitresses.

'I hear from one of your colleagues that I nearly lost you your job. I am very sorry, Noelle. I liked you very much, and that is the truth. It is also the truth that I wanted to make love to you, *elskling.* I am also sorry that you have such high morals. One day you will meet a man – have you perhaps met him already? – who will change all that, I am convinced. But it is plain I am not that man! One day, perhaps, you will come north and meet my family. As I told you, we would give you a good welcome. Just keep going north, almost as far as you can go before you fall into the Arctic Ocean, and you will find the Olsen family waiting for you in North Cape! I shall not forget you. *På gjensyn* – I'll be seeing you. Einar.'

Noelle folded the note and pushed it into her pocket. It was almost a testimonial, she thought wryly, to her principles and a confirmation of her innocence of the intrigue in which Per Arneson was convinced she had been involved. If she showed it to him, would he believe her story? But she would never let him see it. He had no interest in her now, not even as an employee.

Per went away again. It was almost a relief to go into Per's apartment with Kirsten and know that she need not brace herself to meet Kirsten's brother. All the same, she looked for him, feeling his presence in his absence, half afraid, half longing that he would walk out of his room. She listened for his voice and for his footsteps, but they did not come.

Kirsten said she had some spare material she would sell to Noelle if she liked it enough. 'It would make you a good pair of pants. It's scarlet. Do you fancy scarlet trousers?'

Noelle said she needed cheering up and what better than a pair of scarlet trousers? 'I could use my denim jeans as a pattern. They're over in my room.'

Together they went across to the staff house and Noelle let Kirsten into her room. 'Your brother's room, really,' Noelle said, with a sigh. 'I'm sure he regrets ever letting me occupy it.'

Kirsten, who had heard the story of her dismissal and immediate reinstatement, said, 'My brother is quite unscrupulous. He believes what he wants to believe. There are times when it's impossible to get through to his reasonable side. He has one,' with a smile, 'although you may not believe it.' She sauntered round the room, opening cupboards and drawers containing Per's clothes. 'He hasn't left much room for your belongings, has he?'

'Enough,' Noelle commented, raking in a small wardrobe and pulling out a pair of jeans. 'These are the ones I shall use as a pattern.'

She spread the material on the floor and arranged the jeans over it. 'Just enough fabric. I'll take it. How much do you want?'

Between them they decided on a price and Kirsten wandered round again. She turned the handle of the bathroom door. 'This is locked!'

Noelle nodded, folding the material and putting her jeans away. 'Your brother told me it wouldn't be fair to the other members of staff if he allowed me all the "home comforts". That is, a private bathroom as well as a bedroom to myself.'

'*Min gnitne bror!* How could he be so mean! I know where he keeps the key. I shall get it for you.'

'No, Kirsten.' Noelle put out her hand. 'Don't bother, please. Suppose he discovers I've been using the bathroom?'

'He's away, isn't he? You can use it while he's away. I'll not tell him. He will never know, Noelle. How can he? As soon as he returns, you stop using it – or only use it when you know he will not find out, like first thing in the morning, or late at night.'

'But he'll see the key has gone.'

'He won't even notice.' And she was off to Per's apartment for the key.

'Here you are.' She opened the bathroom door, making a face. 'It needs an airing. I'll open a window. There is a shower, too.'

Noelle admired the yellow suite, the yellow-tiled walls, the chrome fittings. Around the shower, with its tiled floor, was a white translucent curtain. She sighed. 'It will be heaven to come in here whenever I want to, instead of beating the others to the bathroom along the corridor and having them hammer on the door if I'm in there too long!'

'Good. Now you are happy. Now you can pretend you're on holiday, instead of here to work all the time.'

'That,' said Noelle ruefully, 'is something I mustn't forget if I want to keep on the right side of your brother.'

Kirsten glanced at her covertly. 'Relations between you are not too good?'

For a moment Noelle did not answer, and when she did, she merely shook her head.

'So his charm for once is not working, eh? So I shall win my bet?'

This time Noelle did not even shake her head in reply.

It was a luxury using Per's bathroom. Noelle revelled in its warmth, its shining fitments, the heated towel rail and the glass shelves. She tried to remember not to leave her talc and make-up in there, in case she had to lock the door quickly, pretending she had not used it.

Mark Anderson attached himself to her again. They walked along the fjord in the evening sun as it sparkled on the water. The tourists came by the coach load, filling the hotels and buying eagerly from the shops.

After Einar, Noelle found Mark uncomplicated. He was dull and self-effacing, but unlike Einar he was predictable. Whenever Mark was by her side, Noelle felt she had the situation under control, even when he kissed her. Now and then they would walk hand in hand. Noelle did not mind. If it pleased Mark, and he made no greater demands, how could she object? They talked about their future careers, about where they would go for their holidays next year.

Noelle left Mark earlier than usual one evening. There would be time for a shower before going to bed. He came with her to the door of her room and pulled her towards him by the shoulders. His kisses were gentle, asking no response. People went up and down the stairs, but Mark was unaware of it and Noelle did not care. Wasn't she behaving like all the other girls she worked with? Kissing her boy-friend good night? Except she had to admit, that there the similarity stopped. They kissed their boy-friends good night on the other side of the door.

When Mark left, Noelle prepared for her shower, pushing her hair into a waterproof cap and pulling the curtain around the shower. While she was washing, someone came in. She did not usually lock the door, except when she was in bed.

'Kirsten?' she called. 'Won't be long. I've cut out the jeans. I'll show them to you.' The noise of the running, splashing water drowned any reply Kirsten had made

Noelle towelled herself briskly and reached outside for the bath robe – presumably Per's – which was hanging there. She tied it round her waist and pushed back the curtain. A gasp came from her throat and her hand lifted protectively to it.

It was not Kirsten who had come in. Standing in the bedroom and watching her through the open door of the bathroom was Per Arneson. The colour washed over her when she remembered that the shower curtain, being semi-transparent, must have hidden very little from Per's gaze. She remembered his words when he had allowed her to use his bedroom. 'The bathroom door is locked. In fairness to the others, it will have to remain locked.' She had broken another of his rules – and he had caught her in the act!

In his palm he tossed a key, to one of the private cupboards, she guessed, which he had probably come to open. His other hand was pushed into a pocket and his manner was seemingly relaxed. Only his eyes, like frosted glass, told her of the cold anger he was feeling.

'Who gave you permission to use my private bathroom?'

Noelle wrapped her arms about her so tightly it was difficult to breathe. Her shoulders were thrust forward in an effort to stop herself from shaking. One more transgression, he had said, and that would be the last . . .

He persisted, 'On whose authority did you use my bathroom, after I had told you not to?'

Noelle was silent. She could not implicate Kirsten, but her loyalty to her friend was wasted.

'Only one person here knows where the key to that bathroom is kept. So it's Kirsten I have to thank for conniving with you to override my directive?' He came towards her slowly, his eyes raking her, a smile without humour but with something else, something which had Noelle's heart racing, lifted the corners of his mouth.

Then it held a touch of malice. 'What would you give me, Miss Roberts, if I allowed you to continue to use this bathroom? Would you give me what you gave Einar Olsen? Would you give me what every woman can give a man?'

Slowly his hands moved towards her. The shower cap was tugged from her head, letting her hair spring free. A hand forced down the shoulder of the robe and his mouth sought the softness of her skin. Then she was in his arms, crushed against him. His lips found hers as though they knew the way blindfold, parting them and forcing back her head. The robe was loosened by the pressure of his body and he sought with his lips the smoothness of her shoulder.

It was useless fighting the desire he was arousing. It was useless fighting him any more. She was helpless in his arms and she clung to him as if she would not let him go. She whispered his name until his bruising mouth stopped the murmur. Then he disengaged her from him and held her away, looking at her parted lips, the colour in her face, the brightness of her eyes.

He did not attempt to touch her again. Instead he smiled, a slow, lazy, infinitely satisfied smile. He gave a low, mocking bow.

'Thank you, Miss Roberts. The bathroom – and the robe,' she drew it closer around her, 'are yours. You've earned them.'

He went out.

CHAPTER EIGHT

NOELLE did not meet Per again for a few days, although she caught occasional glimpses of him in his office behind the reception desk. He did not attend for dinner in the hotel dining-room, nor did he appear when she went with Kirsten to his flat.

Once he happened to look up as she passed across the hotel foyer on her way to the staff house. Even through the window of his office she could see that his face was serious, but there was a narrow, reminiscing look in his eyes which had her remembering, too. Remembering his kisses, the touch of his hands persuading away all resistance and supplanting it with a wish to please, to submit . . .

Yes, she could say to Kirsten, if she asked her now, the charm had worked. It had worked so effectively that it frightened her. The emotions which he evoked in her, and which would not be pacified except by his touch, had no future. As far as he was concerned, she was here in his life for a few more weeks. After that she would go out of his mind as if she had been less than a passing shadow.

Mark's attentions were almost a salve – to her hurt feelings – hadn't Per taken her up, used her and dropped her again? To her pride – hadn't he humiliated her that evening by forcing her to reveal how deeply she felt for him?

Mark had become her slave, waiting for her to go off duty, waiting while she dressed for the evening walk. It was well into August now, and the weather had grown more variable. In the evenings, Noelle appreciated the warmth of the sweater Per had bought her. And she could swear the snow on the mountains across the fjord had deepened and widened.

Kirsten confirmed that it had. 'It's a long way up,' she had said, smiling. 'And it's cold up there. Per has a place half-way up one of those mountains,' she waved across the water. 'It's accessible by car, although you have to walk the final part of the way. He has never taken a woman up there, apart from me and I've only been once – on sufferance! In the winter, he goes up there to ski. In the summer, he escapes to his little wooden house – although it's being kind to call it that. It's really little more than a large hut. He lives there alone for days.'

Odd, Noelle thought, the feeling she experienced when Kirsten told her this. Was she *jealous* of the solitude he seemed to enjoy so much? He could cut himself off, away from all other human contact, withdraw into himself, feeding on his own inner resources without, as it were, a backward glance at all the people he was leaving behind? Did no one have first place in his life next to himself? No woman – not even Sonja Linde?

For a moment, Noelle allowed herself to be just a little sorry for Sonja, then jealousy closed down, shutting out all compassion. Sonja loved the man she loved, and Sonja was therefore her enemy. Neither of them was likely to win in the strange, shadowy battle for Per's love. But at least Sonja was his equal in status and intellect. And she had only to put her arms round his neck – it seemed she had that right although she did not wear his ring – and he would respond immediately in a very masculine way.

Kirsten invited Noelle to dine at Per's apartment one evening. 'I shall cook the meal, you shall be the guest.'

'You mean,' Noelle asked, frowning, 'just the two of us?'

'Per will be here. He says the one thing he doesn't object to about me is my cooking!'

Noelle thought, dine as one of the family, with Per sitting at the table secretly laughing at her? Or perhaps resenting her presence, but being too polite to say so, therefore enduring it in silence?

'It's kind of you, Kirsten, but – well, I shall be on duty—'

'Oh, I'll get you off it. I'll speak to Per.'

'I – don't think your brother will make any more concessions where I'm concerned, Kirsten.'

But Per did, giving instructions to the head waiter to find a substitute for Noelle just for one evening.

'Wear something nice,' Kirsten had said.

But Noelle told her she had brought only informal clothes from England.

'Borrow one of my dresses.' Kirsten had taken from the wardrobe a yellow halter-necked dress with a long, clinging skirt and unbelievably little material above it.

Now, looking at her reflection, Noelle was dismayed to see how much of her was visible – her back to the waist, while at the front little was left to the imagination. Why, she asked herself, had she agreed to borrow it? Kirsten could wear such a dress with panache. She, Noelle, would have been far happier designing such a garment for someone else, kneeling on the floor and cutting it out, sewing it lovingly and seeing it come to life in her hands. Anything but wear it, and in Per's presence . . .

'Come early,' Kirsten had invited, 'and have a drink before dinner. If you get no reply, come round the back. We shall probably be sitting outside watching the sun go down behind the mountains.'

Mark accompanied Noelle to the door of the apartment. When, as Kirsten had predicted, there was no reply, he walked with her round the side of the hotel and along the paved walk near the edge of the fjord towards the swimming pool. Kirsten and her brother were not sitting outside. Kirsten was in the pool, but she saw Noelle and shouted a welcome. Per climbed up the steps and reached for his towel.

He looked narrowly at Noelle's escort, giving him a curt nod, at which Mark squeezed Noelle's hand and sauntered away.

Having disposed with a look of his guest's unwanted admirer, Per turned his attention to the guest herself. As he towelled his gleaming body, he looked her over unsparingly.

His eyes lingered on her bare shoulders, on her arms, on the uncovered expanse from armpits to waist, on the daring neckline.

Noelle gazed back at him, responding with a touch of anguish to his breadth, his height, the firm strength of him.

Kirsten climbed out of the pool, pulling off her cap and wrapping her towel around her. 'If you'd been a bit earlier,' she said, 'you could have joined us.' She sprinted after her brother through the open door into the apartment, calling over her shoulder, 'Drinks are on the table. Help yourself. Give me three minutes.'

She was back in five, wearing a long black skirt and pink evening top. 'You look so good, Noelle. Doesn't she, Per?'

He came to the door of his room, pulling on his shirt and fastening the buttons. It was the translucent shirt which Noelle had seen him wear before, and it showed every movement of his muscles beneath it. The pull of him was like a feast to a starving beggar and it was as much as she could do to stop her eyes from following him. He smiled as if he knew exactly how she was feeling.

He did not answer the question his sister had asked. Instead he said, 'Your own design, Miss Roberts? You made that dress yourself?'

'*Tosk*!' said his sister. 'Fool! It's my dress and Noelle has borrowed it. Don't you recognize it?'

'Not at all,' he drawled. 'I don't look at my sister as I look at other women. And you cannot deny it, there is, at this moment, a great deal of your friend to look at.' His eyes wandered lazily over the revealing areas to which he was referring, then turned back into his room to finish dressing.

Kirsten tossed her head as if despairing of her brother, and went into the kitchen, telling Noelle to find a chair.

'The smell at least,' said Per, coming back into the room, 'is delicious, whatever the food itself might taste like.'

As he walked across to the dining area where the table

was set with place mats and glinting cutlery, he took matches from his pocket and put a flame to the four candles in a silver holder. Since his back was to her, Noelle allowed her eyes to follow him, her heart not far behind. His suit was white, his tie dark blue. His fair hair gleamed in the candlelight and his face as he turned, was smiling.

He approached Noelle as she sat on the couch, and as he came nearer she saw that his smile was speculative more than amused. He subjected her again to his appraisal and the poise with which she had so desperately cloaked herself slipped from her like the seventh veil.

'You know,' he murmured, 'a man can't keep his eyes off you, dressed as you are. You suggest so many things. Warmth – it's in your eyes. Passion – which I know you possess.' He sat beside her, half-turning so that he could watch her. 'Love,' he continued, lowering his voice, 'far into the night.'

The sun had withdrawn its heat and its light into hiding behind the mountains, leaving shadows in the darkening room. The candles, taking over, flickered on the table, their flames a darting, twisting reflection in Per's musing eyes.

His look made her breathing quick and shallow. His hand lifted and came caressingly to rest on the bareness of her shoulder. His fingers feathered down her arm until they reached her wrist. If they rested there, he would feel the thudding of her pulse. She wrenched her wrist away.

He laughed with enjoyment, like an animal stalking its prey and slowly, surely, forcing it into a corner. 'So you will not let me seduce you? Never mind,' he glanced at his watch, 'the night is very, very young. And,' he stood, towering over her, 'I have not yet met a woman who, when I have asked, has said "no".'

Noelle moved with impatience, with anger – with despair. He said, 'You think I say that out of conceit? No, I merely speak the truth.'

Of course he was speaking the truth, how could she doubt it? Looking at him now, he had only to crook his finger and she would go to him, regardless of the consequent and inevitable rejection which, when he had finished with her, would surely follow.

He hitched himself next to her on the arm of the couch. He was crowding her in, but she had no power to move away. As she raised her head, she saw that he was gazing down at her bemusedly. 'No wonder,' he said softly, 'Mark Anderson follows you around like a little pet – yes, I have watched him. No wonder Einar Olsen locked you with him in his room for two nights. How did you enjoy his lovemaking?'

Now she did move away, angrily. 'I couldn't tell you since I didn't experience it. You've—' She checked herself.

'I've – what?'

She had to answer. 'You have kissed me more than he did.'

Per's head went back and he laughed. 'Ah, but,' after a few moments, 'there is more to lovemaking than kissing, as you should know by now.'

'Will you believe me,' she returned furiously, 'when I say that Einar didn't—'

'No, I won't believe you. I know my fellow-men too well, especially my fellow-countrymen, and especially one as experienced and determined as Einar Olsen, to believe that he let such an opportunity pass without extracting something worthwhile from it.'

Kirsten came in, carrying steaming dishes which were giving out an appetizing smell. 'But I told you, *kjære bror,* when you two first met, that Noelle's morals were impeccable, that she was incorruptible.'

Per was amused, deeply and sardonically amused. He turned round. 'You, *min kjære söster,* do not know what you are talking about.'

'Why, do you?' The sharp question had brother and sister looking at each other. Their eyes conducted a silent conversation from which Noelle was entirely excluded. In the end, Kirsten's eyes fell away from Per's and she said no more. It seemed that he had told her wordlessly that his private life was not a subject for public discussion.

After the meal, they drank their coffee in the living area, Kirsten and Noelle on the couch, Per wandering restlessly round the room. He tipped his coffee down his throat, then moved to the windows and drew aside one of the curtains. 'Come here, Noelle,' he said. She rose and went to his side. 'See the mountains in the moonlight? The moon on the snow? You should see it at close quarters as I do when I go to my log cabin high in the mountains. There's a river very near and in the night you can hear it flowing by. Before you go, I will take you there. Would you come? You must get near to the heart of my country instead of always, as it were, skimming the surface.'

'You're asking a *woman,* Per, to your secret hideaway?' Kirsten asked behind them. 'You're honoured, Noelle. There can be only one reason—'

Her brother swung round. '*Vær stille!*' he admonished.

Kirsten said sarcastically, 'In case you have not guessed, Noelle, Per is telling me to shut up.'

Per asked, ignoring her, 'Well, Noelle?'

A little at a loss, Noelle replied, 'Well, I . . . If you really want me to.' Her voice trailed away doubtfully.

'You can be sure,' Per said dryly, 'that if I did not, I would not have asked. As Kirsten says, it's rare indeed that I allow a woman to put a foot inside my hiding place. So you will come.' He closed the curtains and turned away. For him, the matter also was closed.

He put on a record and helped himself to a drink, standing broodingly listening to the sound. Then he downed the liquid, put down his glass and stood in front of Noelle. He did not ask, he pulled her up and into his arms.

With his cheek against her hair, he said one word. 'Dance.'

Kirsten eyed them, half amused. 'I know when I'm – how do the French say it? – *de trop*, one too many. I shall go to the bar. The field is clear for you, brother, to win your bet. The stage is set for the great seduction scene. When I return, I shall creep in. If there is silence and your door is closed, I'll understand. You will have made yet another conquest.'

Per snapped at his sister, '*Gå bort!* Take yourself and your caustic tongue out of here.'

'Noelle,' Kirsten said, 'if you require my help, I shall not be far away. *Lykke til,* Per! You'll need all the good luck you can get.' She opened the door. 'You see, I know Noelle better than you!'

Except for the sound of the music, there was silence. They danced on and now and then Per's lips strayed to Noelle's cheek. Her legs felt weak as a newborn baby's.

'Link your hands round my neck,' he murmured. She obeyed. 'Now I shall hold you like this.' His hands clasped low at her back. 'Now we are close,' he pressed her hips against him, 'really close.' For a long time they danced that way until their footsteps slowed and stopped. 'Kiss me, Noelle,' he commanded, his lips brushing hers.

Noelle told herself he was playing with her, but she was beyond caring. She kissed him gently, uncertainly, until he took over and bruised her mouth with his.

The music finished and he led her to the couch, pulling her beside him. 'This dress of my sister's – there's so little of it, it both delights and lures a man.' The palms of his hands ran lightly up her arms to rest against her throat. He laughed at her attempts to stop him. 'You wouldn't have worn the dress if you hadn't wanted to attract me, to entice me to break through the restraints there have so far been in our relationship.' He lowered his voice. 'You are irresistible, *elskling.* We shall continue from where we left off the other evening, yes? After your shower in my bathroom . . .'

Could she refuse him what he was asking? This was the man she loved. Wasn't it the natural thing to do to show that man her love?

'No, Per,' somehow she had managed to say the word, but only she knew what an effort it cost her.

A quick anger flicked across his eyes. 'Ah, that token resistance again, which no doubt you show to every man who takes an interest in you, merely no doubt to excite them further. So, if that is the way you want it, I shall be further excited.'

He pulled her round until she was lying across him in his arms. His eyes began a journey from her face down her throat to linger intimately on the valley between her breasts. And for once in her life, she did not want to hide her attractions from a man's gaze. His lips rested where his eyes had been.

'Seduction scene,' Kirsten had said with sisterly contempt. 'The stage is set.'

'No, Per,' Noelle whispered, but her voice was feeble.

'Still you say "no", my sweet? My word, you are excitingly different. I have not come across this before.' There was an edge to his voice which made her want to cry. So it *was* a game to him, after all! But had she really been so naïve as to expect otherwise?

'Come, we are wasting time. I have a beautiful woman in my arms. I desire her, so I shall make love to her – like this!'

And his head blotted out the candlelit room, bringing a sighing darkness.

The door handle moved, a switch clicked, the room was flooded with light. They broke apart.

Per swore with violence. 'Get out, Kirsten! Don't you—?'

'*Elskling!*' Sonja put her back to the closed door. 'Darling!'

Per rose, lifting his hands and brushing back his hair. He was in complete command, both of himself and the situation. Noëlle roused herself, sitting up and passing a hand across her eyes, then she lifted them uncertainly to encounter the bitter enmity in Sonja's.

'So, Miss Roberts, you try to take Per Arneson away from me! He is mine, do you hear, he is mine!'

She walked across to Per and fastened her arms round his neck, but he disengaged them at once. 'I belong to no woman, Sonja, not even you.'

'I know differently, *elskling.* Whatever you say, you cannot blot out the memories I have of your kisses.' She glanced maliciously over her shoulder at Noelle.

'Don't worry, Fröken Linde,' Noelle said levelly, rising and straightening her dress, and even as she spoke she wondered at her own self-control, 'I have not taken Per away. I was here, I was near,' the tears rose despite her desperate efforts to suppress them, 'I was used as Per Arneson uses all women. For his own selfish purpose!'

As she ran blinded by tears, across the road to the staff house, she narrowly missed being run down by a car.

'I'm leaving, Noelle,' Mark Anderson said a few days later.

'Going home, Mark?'

'Yes, but before that I'm seeing a bit more of Norway.' They shook hands and exchanged addresses, but Noelle knew she would never see him again.

It was the end of August. How much longer would she stay in Norway herself? Three weeks, no more. Then she would pack her rucksack and go away, travelling alone, because Kirsten would be finding a job in her own country.

Dispiritedly she went about her work. Per had become a bent head in the office, a figure walking briskly at the other end of a corridor, a man – remote and reserved – to be waited on at table.

One day he caught her as she was leaving the hotel to go across to the staff house. 'Your time with us is nearly over?' he asked.

'Two more weeks.'

'This coming week-end I shall be going to my place in the mountains. Will you come?'

So he had remembered! 'Don't worry,' he added with a mocking smile, 'I know what you are thinking, but it will only be for the day. I have no other ideas in mind. We would lunch on the way and I would return you here late at night.'

Her heart leapt at the invitation. Then, 'If – if you really want me to—?'

'You said that before. Let's say I dislike breaking promises. Well, will you come?'

So he did not really want her company, it was his conscience troubling him. All the same she said, 'I should like to very much.'

He said sarcastically, 'You are sure I don't intend to use you "for my own selfish purpose"?'

She coloured and looked down. 'I'm sorry.'

'Don't apologize. Who knows, you may have been right!' He returned to his office, saying, 'I will tell you the arrangements nearer the time.'

When they started on their journey into the mountains, the day looked promising, but as time went by clouds began to collect overhead.

'Will it snow?' Noelle asked, a little anxious.

Per lifted a careless shoulder, taking his eyes momentarily from the road and scanning the sky. 'I doubt it. But I think it will rain before long.'

As they drove, after lunching at a large, modern hotel overlooking a great plunging gorge, their conversation was impersonal. He told her about the chalet he owned some distance from Bergen.

'It's built of wood as nearly all of them are. Wood is cheap and plentiful in our country. The chalet has a small kitchen, but a large dining-room. Like most of the others, it has a *peisestue*, an open-hearth fire, built up with logs. Translated literally, it means fire room, that is, where everyone gathers round the fire. Upstairs there are two bedrooms and a bathroom. It's very comfortable and, unlike my mountain retreat where we're going, has all the modern conveniences. All around there are chalets of different design, like Canadian Rockies log cabins, or chalets at Austrian ski resorts.'

'It sounds as if a lot of people own places like that. Do they live there all the time?'

'Not usually. They are used as holiday homes, or places to go for the week-end. You see, Norwegians tend to live in flats, apartments, more than houses. House ownership is rarer here than in Britain.'

'Kirsten told me you ski a lot in winter.'

He nodded. 'Sometimes I stay with my parents in Oslo, or at a ski resort fifteen hundred feet up, that is, as we measure it in Norway, roughly four hundred and ninety metres. I join friends there,' he flicked her a smile, 'one or two of them are Olympic champions. We take part in winter sports and ski to our hearts' content.'

Noelle, gazing out at the brooding mountains, had a fleeting vision of Per in ski suit, complete with goggles, skimming expertly over the snow, down the slopes and out of her imagination – and her life. He spoke of an existence of which she could not even dream because she had no knowledge, no personal experience of it. And had she, in her secret mind, cherished a hope that one day he might come to love her as she loved him? A man with his possessions, his influence and his fortune?

The gathering clouds were thickening and she wondered if Per had noticed. Watching his frowning face stare at the sky through the windscreen, she guessed he had.

'I had hoped to stay here until evening,' he said. 'Those are storm clouds. Unfortunately, I think they may drive us down again before dark.'

'Is it a chalet we're going to?' Noelle asked.

He laughed. 'Far from it. It's a log cabin with a roof made of turf, for greater protection. It stands in a clearing. Years ago the trees were felled and the space left open to keep the wolves away from the cattle. It's a kind of "back to nature" place. I keep it that way. I could have had it modernized and a generator installed to provide electricity, but I have not, for the simple reason that when I come here, I do so to get away from everything,' he shot her a laughing glance, 'even civilized behaviour.'

'But,' she asked uncertainly, 'how do you cook, keep the place clean?'

Momentarily he lifted his hands from the steering wheel. 'With these. How else? And there's a small range – called a *komfyr* – for cooking, plenty of fuel in the form of logs. You see,' with a mocking smile, 'I'm not the eternal, the complete playboy. There are other, better sides to my nature than you seem to believe.'

She responded bitterly, 'For fun you live as the poor are forced to live every day. You have so much money, so many material possessions, you have to get away from them and escape into pretended deprivation and poverty – as a diversion.'

'So,' he had become a little pale under his deep tan, 'you think even worse of me than I realized.'

Her eyes clung to the wild beauty of the landscape, seeing how the heather bloomed on the hills, its colour a vivid contrast to the gentle greens around it. If I could tell you, she thought, how I have placed you above all men, how the other men I know look puny beside you . . .

He negotiated one of a series of hairpin bends and Noelle found herself afraid to look down the precipitous slope of the land on one side of them and up at the towering cliffs on the other.

The skill with which Per drove in such perilous conditions had her breathless with admiration. She must, in fact, have held her breath because he said, with a smile, 'I'll take a guess – you're terrified.'

She could only nod.

'Relax. I've made this journey so many times I could almost do it blindfold, hairpin bends included!'

So Noelle did relax, as far as the sheer drops to the right or to the left would let her. The road had been blasted out of the rock, but below them was rock, too, and as if that were not enough, across the narrow gorge the mountains towered, grained and creviced and twisted as though a giant hand had had its way. Pine trees lined the lower slopes, and here and there bushes and small trees sprang valiantly from such patches of fertile soil as existed in the crevices.

'Do you,' she asked after a while, 'own the log cabin we're going to?'

'No, it belongs to my uncle who lives in Trondheim. He was a farmer but has now retired. Once he had a herd of cows and, like many farmers, owned a series of such cabins placed at intervals on the mountainside. In the summer, dairymaids lived in these cabins.'

'Not surely on their own?'

He nodded. 'But they are not lonely because around them, not so far away are other dairymaids in cabins owned by other farmers. They are all friendly.'

'But what do they do with themselves all day?'

'Plenty of things. One cow in the herd wears a bell and at milking time that cow makes its way down the hillside to the cowshed below the living quarters. The rest of the herd follows. The dairymaid milks them and turns them loose again. At the end of the day, the cows return and stay in the shed for the night. In between times, the dairymaid makes butter and so on. When the pasture around that particular cabin is used up, there is another log cabin about an hour's walk higher up the mountain, so the dairymaid moves up there, taking the herd with her.'

'Surely they don't live there in the winter, too?'

'No, much too exposed. Norwegian winters are wintry indeed, so in the winter the cabins are empty, the cows come down into the valleys. There's a tale my uncle tells about a dairymaid who, a long time ago, called the goat in to be milked. It knew its name and obeyed the summons. She proceeded to milk the goat in the old-fashioned way with her hands into a bucket. The goat swung its tail and it went into the milk. Being a thrifty young woman, what did the dairymaid do but wring out the goat's tail over the bucket, letting the milk run back to join the rest!'

Noelle laughed. 'I can hardly believe it.'

'My uncle swears it's true. It was many years ago, of course.'

'Will there be a dairymaid at the cabin today?' Noelle asked.

Per laughed. 'No, I told you my uncle has retired. But anyway, he, like other farmers, is finding it more profitable these days to let these cabins to tourists.' He looked at his watch. 'Not long now. I think we'll make it before the rain comes.'

They did, but with little time to spare. Per explained that he would have to park the car on the other side of the river. There was a footbridge, he explained, which they would have to cross to get to the cabin.

Soon they reached a plateau and Per raised his arm, pointing. 'There's the cabin, across the river.'

It was smoother going, and up here the land was green. Sheep grazed, cows wandered and the atmosphere was one of uninterrupted peace.

'It's a pity,' said Per, 'you're not seeing it in sunlight. But those clouds up there mean business, business they will transact before very long!'

The road became little more than a track and Per pulled the car in to a parking place which had been created, it seemed, especially for that purpose.

Only the river now lay between them and the cabin, a rushing, frothing, cascading river, passing near the cabin which stood on higher ground.

'That water,' Per indicated the river, 'is icy cold. It comes down from the mountains. The glaciers melt and run into it. I wouldn't advise you to swim in it, but for drinking it's unsurpassable. It's like wine but better.'

The 'bridge' to which Per had referred consisted only of three long, stout tree trunks bound together and spanning the water.

'We have to cross that?' Noelle asked, her eyes wide.

Per laughed. 'Why not? Come, give me your hand. There is room for two to cross at once.'

So, with her hand in Per's, she allowed herself to be led over the river to the safety of the other bank.

The cabin was two-storeyed with a shallow, sloping roof. At ground level was the cowshed and it seemed to be where Per stored some of his possessions. Skis leant against a wall, a sledge lay in a corner. There were piles of logs, too, and Noelle supposed Per had sawn them himself.

The wooden steps leading up to the living quarters were outside the building. Per went up first, opening the door with a key.

The room they entered had a few home comforts, but few enough to be counted on one hand – a couple of rocking chairs, a rough wooden table with matching benches on each side, a bookcase, the shelves tightly packed. At one end was the cooking range Per had mentioned. The fire had been laid and as Per put a match to it, an acrid smell of burning wood filled the room.

He opened a cupboard and then another. In one was a black and white ski suit swinging on a hanger, with leather gloves and goggles on a shelf. In the second cupboard was climbing equipment, boots with crampons; rods and lines for fishing.

Without warning it grew dark and the rain began. It pelted on the windows and on the wooden walls of the cabin.

'Don't look so scared,' Per said. 'I have a stock of water in.'

'Water?' Noelle looked round. 'No taps?'

'No wash basin, either. Over there,' he indicated a chest of drawers, 'is a bowl. I wash in that. I get buckets of water from the river and heat it on the fire. But don't worry,' with a smile, 'I have one luxury. I've been civilized enough to have a toilet installed!' He opened a trapdoor in the floor and a ladder led to the cowshed below. 'It's down there. Don't frown like that.' He smiled. 'It's quite private, with a door.'

He lit an oil lamp and then another, and the smell caught at the nostrils. The lamps cast a flickering, yellow, hissing glow and Noelle noticed that their shadows, her and Per's, having none of the inhibitions of the substance, merged intimately on the floor of the room.

'It sounds as if you live like a hermit.'

'I told you,' with a smile, 'here I retreat into myself, find myself again. Apart from my family, you are the only woman I have ever brought here.'

'Should I thank you?'

He smiled at her smiling, upraised face. 'I think you should. Today I have conferred a privilege, an honour on you. I have, as it were, let you into part of me.'

The words sounded so personal, so intimate, so private, such an incredible concession on his part they almost put her under an obligation to thank him in whatever way he might ask of her. Almost as if he could read her mind, as though her thoughts echoed what might have been in his, he nodded towards the bunk beds tucked away in a corner of the room.

'Go and inspect them. They're comfortable enough once you get used to two-tiered sleeping.'

She felt them and they gave under the pressure of her hand. All the same, she was puzzled. After the supreme comfort of his flat and even his room in the staff house, this place was almost stark. How such a man, with his expensive habits, with his worldliness and his – she could not overlook the fact – his desires, could adapt to such an ascetic, solitary way of life, she simply could not grasp.

It showed her a side of him that daunted her, intimidated and dismayed her. Because now she not only loved him, she had to respect him, too. She had to put aside her secret contempt for his playboy image, a contempt which had helped to keep in check her feelings for him. Now there was no barrier, nothing to hold back the force of those feelings, nothing to prevent the deepening and consolidation of her love. It meant, also, that she would have to strengthen her resolve, her determination to withstand his approaches, his persuasiveness, his charm.

'You seem puzzled about something.' He was leaning against the wall, hands in pockets, legs casually crossed. He had removed his parka and his white sweater seemed to be the twin of the one she was wearing and which he had given her. The high turn-over collar framed his face, accentuating its fine bone structure, the ice blue of his eyes – today the ice had melted – and the rich fairness of his hair.

Her resolution was crumbling, there was no doubt about it. She wanted to stand in front of him until those arms wrapped about her. She replied, 'I – I suppose it's adequate for a holiday.'

'For the sort of holiday I take here, it's just fine. Does the place appeal?'

How would he react if she replied, If you were here to share it with me, it would be heaven on earth. 'I love it,' she said aloud. 'But it doesn't somehow add up to you, Per Arneson, business tycoon, property owner, rich and pampered man.'

He laughed loudly. 'You know so little about me, Noelle, so very little.' He walked across the living-room and looked through the window. 'The rain is lighter. I have some fresh stores in the car. Would you mind if I leave you to get them? Make yourself comfortable. Behave as if you were in your own home. Imagine,' he said, smiling broadly, 'you're primitive woman to my primitive man.'

She went to the window and watched him go down the wooden stairs to the ground. As he crossed the bridge, she wondered whether or not it was her imagination that the river was flowing faster than when they had arrived. As Per had said, the rain had eased a little, but the clouds were low enough to form patches of swirling mist. Noelle tried to quell her anxiety. Per knew the area blindfold, he had told her, in which case he would surely be able to make the journey back, whatever the weather.

On the windowsill and on a small table covered with a cloth there were photographs. There, surely, was Kirsten as a small girl, Kirsten as a teenager, Per as a student, Per with his arm round Sonja Linde. In his eyes, was she so much one of the family that her portrait appeared among them? There were two older people, standing in front of a wooden house – no doubt the chalet which Per owned – arms round each other – smiling at the camera. They were in their fifties, Noelle guessed, and were almost certainly Per's and Kirsten's parents.

The man was tall, his bearing commanding, but Per, Noelle decided, had the look of his mother about him, although there was a hardness in his features she certainly did not possess. She looked a delightful person and Noelle sighed, thinking how good it might have been to have met them one day.

Per kicked the door open and came in, arms filled with a large box which he lowered to the table.

'It looks,' said Noelle, 'as if you were intending to stay for a week, instead of a few hours.'

'A week.' He eyed her speculatively. 'That's an idea.'

Noelle put up her hands to hide her face. 'Don't look at me.'

He sighed. 'The woman does not seem to have the word "yes" in her vocabulary. Perhaps if I tell her what it is in Norwegian, she might say it. It's *ja,* Noelle. Say it.'

She laughed and shook her head, and Per tutted. 'I cannot even catch her out that way. Never mind, I refuse to give up trying.'

He unloaded the box over the table. 'We will not starve. We shall have our own private *smörgåsbord*, our cold table. Here we have disposable plates, disposable cups, a bottle of wine, milk, coffee. Sit down, Noelle, and I shall wait on you.' His eyes twinkled. 'That will make a change, will it not? Now, shall I argue with you, as you argue with your customers, including your boss, spill the soup over you which I'm going to warm at the fire?' He smiled wickedly and she almost felt the need to apologize all over again.

The fire which heated the cooking range roared, sending out its pleasant woody smell. The heat beckoned and Noelle curled up on the rug in front of it. As Per opened tins, produced cheeses and cold meats, tomatoes and ham and crispbread, Noelle asked him if he had any means of communicating with the outside world.

'No telephone,' he replied, 'nothing. Here I'm incommunicado. No television, either, not even a portable one. I do have a transistor radio which works reasonably well, despite the mountains around. But I rarely have it on. Now you're going to ask me, What do you do with yourself? I read, I fish in the river, I go for walks high up into the mountains.' A pause. 'I find myself again.'

Noelle closed her eyes. How little need he had of other people! Would any woman penetrate the barricade he had constructed around himself, his innermost person? His self-sufficiency was so complete she was convinced no woman – not even Sonja – could ever become a necessary and integral part of his happiness.

They ate their meal in front of the fire, with the radio playing in the background. They talked about Noelle's studies at college in dress design. He spoke of his family and she asked about the age gap between himself and his sister.

'My parents were under twenty when they married. When I was born, they realized they had their hands full with me and decided to have no other children. Twelve years later – they were still only in their early thirties – Kirsten made her appearance as a result of an impulse on my parents' part.' He glanced at Noelle as she sipped the coffee he had made. 'They loved each other that way.' For a moment he was silent. 'They still do.'

She asked, wondering at her own daring, 'You haven't followed their example and married young?'

'Obviously not.' It was coolly spoken and for the first

time that day Noelle sensed the barriers being raised against her. What had she expected – a detailed account of his private life, his past love affairs?

He broke the silence. 'You must meet my mother and father some time. You would like them.' He glanced at her again. 'And I'm sure that liking would be reciprocated.'

'Thanks, but it's out of the question, isn't it? In roughly two weeks I shall be going home to England.'

He smiled. 'And will you forget me?'

Forget him? Forget the man who meant more to her than any other man alive? She said, in a voice as noncommittal as she could make it, 'Probably.'

The word and the tone aroused him. He got up and came across to her as she moved backwards and forwards in the rocking chair. 'You're a cool customer, aren't you?' His eyes glittered in the lamplight. He took her hand and tugged until she uncurled herself, then he pulled her up. 'I could make you remember me in such a way that you would never forget.' His fist under her chin forced her face up. 'I'm tempted, by heaven I'm tempted. And afterwards, *elskling*,' he whispered, 'you would never want to let me go.'

'You know so much about women, don't you?' she said bitterly. 'You must take them by the dozen and pass on, leaving them littering the wayside.'

He laughed. 'Hardly by the dozen, my sweet. I'm not some kind of superman. One by one, please.'

She hated his mockery and jerked her face from his bruising fingers.

'No, you don't!' His hands pressed each side of her head, forcing her to be still. 'If you escaped from me, how far could you run? Across the room? Give in gracefully, sweet one, admit you're beaten.'

Unexpectedly he reached out and she was in his arms. A hand behind her head forced her mouth on to his. The other hand ran down her back and caressed her hip, pressing her against him. It was her love for him that made her acquiesce as he impelled her down to the rug. Their bodies clung and he said, his voice husky,

'At last you say yes, Noelle? You cannot continue to deny me now. I have explored your shape with my eyes – when you showered in my room behind that revealing curtain—'

So, Noelle thought, he *had* watched her that day!

'Now,' he persisted, 'I want to explore you with my hands, my mouth—'

'Per,' she moaned, 'no, please . . .'

'Are you still denying me that privilege?' His eyes, in the semi-darkness mocked a little. 'You see, I call it a privilege because I still respect you.'

For how long? she thought unhappily. Until it was over, then . . . She turned her face from his approaching mouth, but with compelling fingers he jerked it back.

Into the clamouring silence of the next few moments there was a noise which had Per still and listening. There came from outside the pelting of the rain and the thundering of the river. Per lifted himself from Noelle and went to the window, then to the door, which he opened. The noise became louder, filling the room with a frightening, unrestrained roar. Noelle stood up, pushing her hair from burning cheeks.

Per returned, closing the door, his face serious. 'The bridge is unusable. There must have been a deluge high in the mountains. The river has swollen so much it has become impassable.'

Noelle stared at him. 'So what do we do?'

He shrugged. 'Stay here until the waters subside sufficiently for us to cross the bridge.'

'Which could take how long?'

'Who knows? A day, two days. It depends on when it stops raining, not only here but higher up. In really bad conditions the ground gets bogged and it's impossible to walk on it.'

Noelle turned pale. 'But, Per, we can't stay here.'

'Can't we? What do you suggest we do – swim for it?' She had no answer. 'I have a large stock of wood for the fire and oil for the lamps. There's plenty of food. Plenty of water out there.' He gave a twisted smile. 'You won't even have to share a bed with me – unless you want to. Of course, it will be necessary to share the same room.'

'You mean we sleep on those bunk beds?'

'Where else? You surely don't expect me to act the perfect gentleman and go downstairs to sleep in the cowshed? However, I'll be kind and let you choose which bunk you prefer. But take heart, it's not yet bedtime. There's the radio, books by the dozen. Ourselves.'

The word made her look at him. So, to pass the time, he was suggesting they made love?

But for the remainder of the evening, while the rain drummed on the windows and the swollen river rushed by outside, Per did not touch her. They sat in the rocking chairs in front of the *komfyr* – the cooking range – and read books and magazines. There was music on the radio, interspersed with talking which Noelle could not understand because it was in Norwegian.

Per opened a carton of milk and heated its contents, handing a brimming mug to Noelle. He lifted his in an ironic gesture. 'May we both enjoy our night's sleep.'

A little later Noelle yawned, trying to stifle it, but Per laughed. 'It's no use, Noelle, you'll have to give in. You're tired. You cannot fight that tiredness all night.'

He pulled her from the chair, but she shrank from his touch because of the way it aroused her. He seemed irritated and asked sharply, 'Which bunk do you want, top or bottom?'

'The bottom one, if you don't mind.'

He shrugged. 'I'm asking you. I'm easy either way.'

At her request, he opened the trapdoor and gave her a torch to help her find the way. Soon she was back and asked, 'How do I wash, Per?'

'There's water in a pan on the fire. Pour it into the bowl. You'll find a towel over there. We'll share that.'

'Where do I throw the water away?'

'Outside. I'll do that. Tell me when you've finished with it.' An eyebrow rose. 'Any more questions?'

'Yes. Will you – will you please go away, Per?'

Their eyes met, hers steady, his questioning 'You really want me to?' She nodded. He shrugged and said, lifting the trapdoor, 'I'll descend to the depths. But don't expect me to be away too long, will you?'

Hurriedly she prepared for bed. Under her sweater, which she removed, was a button-through shirt. She undressed to the waist and put a towel round her shoulders. She washed quickly, drying herself. Since she had no nightwear, she decided to wear her shirt and just before she got into bed, she would remove her jeans and sleep in her undergarments. Dreading Per's reappearance too soon, she put down the towel and picked up the shirt from the bunk, slipping her arms into it.

'Noelle.' She spun round. Per was standing in the middle of the room. The colour flooded into her cheeks. How long had he been there? He came towards her and she fumbled with the buttons, managing in her agitated state to match only one button to one buttonhole

As he reached her she backed away, but he followed, taking her by the arms and whispering her name again. She had no defence against him now, but even so she would not give in without a fight.

'No, Per, please—'

'No? *Nei?* What is this word you love so much? So *ja, ja, ja.* Yes, Per, yes. It sounds so much better.' He smiled down at her, shaking his head. 'It's no use, *kjæreste*, I see surrender in your eyes.' His arm, went round her. 'I feel it in your body.' He pulled her to him, crushing her against him, cradling her head, giving her kiss after kiss.

The feel of his body against hers, the urgency within him which grew with his increasing ardour, aroused in her an ecstasy to which she was a total stranger, and like a child in the presence of an unknown person, she grew apprehensive, uneasy and – as the reality of what was happening hit her like a bullet – frightened.

She stiffened, withdrawing into herself, and he lifted his mouth from hers, holding her away. He looked her over indolently. 'What's the matter? You cannot surely be pretending an innocence I know perfectly well you do not possess. No woman could be locked in with a man like Einar Olsen as you were and come out untouched and virtuous.'

'You're wrong!' she cried. 'Einar tried to get me to sleep with him, but he didn't succeed.'

He smiled. 'You don't really expect me to believe that, either, do you, after the way you've been responding so passionately to me this evening? Be honest, my sweet, you want me as much as I want you. You cannot deny it.'

'I do deny it,' she cried, backing away and wrapping the shirt around her. 'You may want me, in fact I know you do, but you want every woman who comes your way. You told me so once. Kirsten said you had an insatiable appetite for the opposite sex. She said it on the ship when I first met you. That's something else I haven't forgotten.'

She stormed on, flinging accusations at him because it was her only form of self-defence, not caring about the anger which was hardening his face and tightening his lips. 'You had a bet with Kirsten. You would use your technique on me, wear me down, get me where you got all women you desire – in your bed. I told you once that I thought you'd exploit any situation – any woman – to the full, provided it was to your advantage. Well, I was right, but you're not going to use me for your own ends as you've used all the other women in your life. One day I'll say "yes" to a man – the man I love,' her voice wavered and steadied, 'and who loves me, too.

'Kirsten told you about my morals, didn't she, the ones you said you would change? Well, she didn't tell you about my pride, but good or bad, I've got it, and I'll not be used by any man, you included, solely as a means of working off his frustrations!' She looked round wildly. 'I'm not staying here with you. I don't trust you not to "try your technique" on me again.' She pushed past him and ran to the door. 'I don't trust you, do you hear?' she cried hysterically, sobbing now. She wrenched the door open.

'Where the hell are you going?'

'Outside,' she shrieked, 'and you can't stop me!'

'You can't go out there, woman. There's all hell let loose!'

But she would not listen. As she stood in the darkness at the top of the flight of steps, listening with horror to the fury of the gale and feeling the pelting of the rain all over her body, the wind caught at her through the thinness of her shirt. She wrapped the material about her, gasping for breath and feeling rather than seeing the thunder of the river as it swirled and foamed and leapt across the bridge.

Per started down behind her and, afraid of what he might do if he caught up with her, Noelle ran down the wooden stairs. Half-way, she tripped and plunged to the ground, hitting the rain-soaked earth and lying stunned and still at the foot.

CHAPTER NINE

'FOR God's sake, Noelle, what have you done?'

For a few moments the rain flung itself against her inert body, then she was lifted and carried upwards, her head sagging, her limbs lifeless. The door was kicked open and she was placed tenderly on the soft-piled rug with a cushion beneath her head.

'Noelle, tell me if I hurt you.' Hands moved along her legs, her arms, all over her, feeling her scalp, testing for serious damage. '*Takk himmelen!*' Per breathed, 'only bruising and abrasions, it seems.'

A towel was drying her, fingers, oddly unsteady, were fastening her shirt. Per went away and Noelle stirred, seeking for him and following him with her eyes. He returned with water, cleaning the blood from a painful place on her temple and applying healing cream and plaster. As he repeated the treatment on her arm and hand, she whispered,

'I'm sorry, Per. I was stupid . . .' But he shook his head and put a finger on her lips.

She touched the side of her head and immediately his fingers probed. 'It hurts?'

She moved her head restlessly. 'It's throbbing.'

'No abrasion,' he commented, 'but there is a bruise already forming.' He smiled. 'Soon you will possess a commendable bump.'

He lifted her again and carried her across the room, putting her on to the lower of the two beds. He removed her shoes and asked, 'You wish to sleep in your jeans? They are mud-stained from your fall.' She shook her head. 'Will you remove them yourself, or—' with a crooked smile, 'will you *trust* me to do it for you?'

She nodded, pressing her lips together and turning away. 'I'm sorry for saying that.'

He unfastened the waistband. 'And I'm sorry for behaving in such a way that you had to say it. Lift up.' She complied and the jeans were slipped off. 'So now we are equal in our sorrow.' He smiled, pulling the soft, expensive quilt over her – the only touch of luxury in the whole place – and smoothed her hair as it spread out on the pillow. 'Now sleep. Later, I shall come to bed.'

There was darkness everywhere when Noelle awoke. Above her was the sound of Per's deep breathing. Outside, the river still frothed and foamed, but there was no rain beating on the windows.

She stirred and the consequent pain immediately reminded her of her injuries. When she remembered where she was and how she came to be there, memories flooded into her mind as fast as the water in the river outside. She stirred even more restlessly.

There was a movement above her head. A torch flashed and Per swung down. 'Something wrong?'

'No,' she whispered, but he struck a match to light the lamp. In its glow he looked down at her.

'Are you in pain?' His fingers touched the plaster on her temple. 'I can give you something to ease it.'

'No, thank you.'

He sat on the bunk beside her. He had not undressed except for removing his sweater. In the half-light she saw that he was smiling. 'Still saying "no",' he teased. 'How tired I am of that little word!'

She smiled up at him, a tremulous, uncertain smile which soon faded. His shirt was open and she wanted to reach out and wrap her arms about him, feeling the soft hairs on that chest against her skin, the hardness of his arms around her.

'What is it, Noelle?' Had he sensed what she was thinking?

Their eyes locked and, mesmerized, she raised a hand to touch him, only to let it fall again before it had even started on its journey. But he picked up that hand and held it against his chest, imprisoning it with both of his.

'Per,' she whispered. The lamplight deepened the fairness of his hair and, unable now to resist the impulse, she lifted her other hand and touched its softness.

He seemed to catch his breath and gathered her into his arms. His hand caressed, bringing her to ecstatic life. There was infinite tenderness in his kiss as well as passion – a controlled passion which nonetheless had her clamouring for more.

But he held her away at last. 'Now she says "yes",' he murmured huskily, 'now, when I have to treat her like Dresden china for fear of hurting her! If that isn't just like a woman!'

'Oh, Per . . .' Her lips trembled and her head turned away.

She was back in his arms. 'No tears, *kjæreste*, my dearest.' He caught her chin and his kiss was gentle. 'Sleep now. I am here above you. If you need me I shall be back again, like that.' He clicked his fingers She turned with difficulty on to her side and he pulled the cover over her. 'The rain has stopped. Even the river has been tamed a little.' He bent down, putting his lips to her ear. 'Like you, *elskling*!'

She smiled up at him. Odd how she did not resent his words. Her eyes closed and a few moments later she was asleep.

It was daylight when Noelle awoke to the fragrance of freshly made coffee. She stirred and the movement made her aware at once of her bruises and the cuts on her face and body. A moan escaped her and Per was there at once, crouching beside her.

'Painful?' he asked, stroking her tousled hair.

She nodded, smiling into his eyes which were level with hers. 'Per?' The word was a question, asking, Is there really something between us? Because of the way you smile at me and worry about me, do I mean more to you than other women? Or is it wishful thinking, that I *want* to believe that? Is it just your conscience causing you to feel guilty about the events leading up to my fall and making you therefore more attentive? Is the way you are kissing me now, gently, tenderly, an apology and a promise that it won't happen again? Can't you see by the way I'm responding that I want it to happen again?

'*Kjæreste*,' he murmured, smiling, 'what are you trying to do – seduce *me* now?'

Embarrassed, she immediately took away her arms. 'No, no! Don't curl up inside at what I said, because it's what I want, darling, what I've been wanting to happen between us all these weeks. Come, kiss me again as you were doing just now.'

And because she loved him so much, she complied. Then he put her back on the pillow. 'Enough. The time, the circumstances are wrong. When you are fit again, perhaps, we will really make love.' He stood, looking down at her. 'And that is a promise I shall keep. Now, do you want help with dressing or—?' She shook her head and he smiled again. 'You have little enough to put on, heaven knows. You see, already I'm beginning to know all about you. Like a lover . . .'

Noelle dressed and washed. When she had finished, Per joined her to shave. Noelle combed her hair and they shared the small mirror on the wall. It was a scene which was as intimate as if they were really lovers. Per had removed his shirt and Noelle saw the toughness of his muscles, the breadth of his back which told of the active life he led both at work and at play, of his climbing and his skiing and his walking for miles high into the mountains.

They breakfasted together on coffee and crispbread and the cold meat left over from their evening meal.

At the window Per said, 'The river has quietened enough for us to be able to cross the bridge if we tread carefully.' He gazed at the sky, still heavy with clouds. 'As long as we pack quickly and go before it rains again.'

It was not long before they were on their way, the perishable foods having been packed into the boot of the car, the remainder left behind for the next visit. Which, Noelle mused sadly, watching the magnificence of the mountain scene in the early morning, Per would be making alone. The weather relented and the sun broke through, rising over the peaks, glinting on the rain-washed snow on the summits and casting great shadows across the valleys.

'Look,' said Per, pointing ahead to where the sunlight reflected, pale yellow, on a patch of the fjord which fingered its way round the base of the pine-covered hills, 'a rainbow. Got your camera?' Noelle twisted round and lifted it from the back seat. 'Catch it quickly before it fades.'

She scrambled out of the car and took the photograph while the prismatic colours arched, each vivid and separate yet merging, from deep in the valley to high over the hills.

She had caught her rainbow. It was safe in her camera and imprinted for all time on her mind. Like the few intimate hours she had spent in Per's company in the log cabin in the mountains, it would never fade. She had caught its image on film to look at, to admire through the years, but never, like the man beside her, to touch.

He told her as they descended into the valley that they would be back at the hotel in time for lunch. Then he would be going away for a few days.

'I should have gone this morning, but other events,' he glanced, smiling, at her, 'prevented me. So I shall go this afternoon.'

She asked, her voice small, forcing out the question, 'How long will you be away?'

He lifted a shoulder. 'Three, four days.'

All that time without him! But even when he came back what would she have? They would return to normal, he to his position as boss, she as his employee. Then in two weeks they would say good-bye. And he wouldn't even notice her going. After all, he had Sonja, to whom he was practically engaged.

'I'm going to Trondheim. One of my hotels is there. I

shall stay with my aunt and uncle, the uncle who owns the cabin in which we have just spent the night.'

At the hotel he parked the car and escorted her to the staff house. 'You're still not fit to return to duty,' he told her. 'Fru Vatne, the *oldfrue*, the housekeeper, will look after you. She has had nursing experience. She'll attend to your bruises and cuts.'

Noelle protested that there was no need and that she was quite able to work, but Per insisted, leaving her in her room to search for the housekeeper. Fru Vatne came bustling along, tutting at the sight of the plaster and bruises on Noelle's face.

'You fell down the steps at the log cabin,' she said. 'Herr Arneson has told me. The storm – was it terrible?'

Noelle nodded, wishing Per had not told the housekeeper so much. He joined them. 'Now, Noelle, you will do as I say and rest until I return. Fru Vatne, Fröken Roberts is not to work, you understand? I will hold you personally responsible for her welfare in my absence.'

Looking a little startled, Fru Vatne nodded. Per caught Noelle's chin and kissed her lingeringly. 'I must go on my way, *kjæreste*. I shall not be away any longer than I need.' He nodded to Fru Vatne who was smiling knowingly as if she understood everything now. After all, hadn't they just spent the night together? But, Noelle, thought despairingly, Fru Vatne didn't know anything, anything at all.

The housekeeper said she would return in a few minutes and discreetly left them. Per turned Noelle to face him.

'Why,' she asked, 'did you have to kiss me like that? Now she'll think we're having an affair.'

He put his arms possessively round her waist. 'You may now know it, *min lille pusekatt*, my little kitten,' he murmured, kissing her nose, 'but we are.' He whispered, 'Be waiting for me when I return, *kjæreste*, I want to talk to you.'

When he had gone, Noelle lay on the bed. The fall at the cabin had shaken her more than she had realized. The presence of Per, the potent quality of his nearness had served to mask the discomfort of her injuries. Now he had gone, there was no barrier to the pain.

There was also another kind of pain. 'I want to talk to you,' he had said. It was only too clear what it was he wanted to say – that he had tired of Sonja Linde and that she should take her place as his next woman. But, loving him as she did, would she have the strength to withstand his request? She sat up painfully. Wasn't she being naïve in thinking there would be a *request*? It would be no such thing. He would start making love to her again and their ultimate coming together as lovers would be as unavoidable and inevitable as the crashing of a car whose brakes had failed and which was speeding towards a brick wall.

It would be a turning-point in her life, an ending and a beginning. To him she would be just another woman. And yet – she swung her legs to the floor and rubbed her hand over her face – he had been so tender in the cabin, so considerate and concerned, so – so loving. She remembered the expression in his eyes each time he had looked at her. The ice had been gone from them for so long now she had almost forgotten how cold they could become. She shivered as if the memory of that ice had the power to chill her.

Fru Vatne, returning, saw it. 'A shower, Fröken Roberts. Then I will dress your wounds.'

Noelle asked, 'Is Kirsten around?'

'Fröken Arneson has gone to visit friends,' Fru Vatne replied. 'But she will return tomorrow. Now you must go in there,' she indicated the bathroom. 'After I have tended your cuts you must rest.'

But when Fru Vatne had gone at last, Noelle did not want to rest. She wandered round the room, part of her longing for Per's instant return, part of her wanting never to see him again.

That evening she was called by Fru Vatne to the phone.

'Noelle? How are you?'

Her pulses leapt. So Per was calling her from his uncle's home. He had not put her out of his mind. Perhaps he was acting the solicitous employer?

'I'm feeling better, thank you,' she replied, the words coming a little breathlessly.

'Is Fru Vatne looking after you, spoiling you? I have given her strict instructions.'

'She's running round me as if I were your – your—' she reproached herself for her indiscretion and hoped he would not pursue the subject.

But he murmured, and she could almost feel the smile on his face, 'You were my what, *elskling*?'

'Your – your woman.'

'But, *kjæreste*, you are, aren't you? Admit that you are.' She was silent. 'Admit it!' he insisted.

'Yes,' she whispered, abandoning herself to the delight of being able to tell him so at last. 'Yes, yes, yes!'

'My own Noelle,' there was a ring of triumph in his voice, 'why do I have to be so far away from you? Why do you have to tell me that when I cannot take you in my arms?' There was a voice in the background. 'I must go. My aunt is calling me to a meal. Good night, my sweet Noelle. I shall be with you soon. Tell me, "Good night, Per, *elskling*". You have heard me say it often enough to know how to pronounce it.'

'Good night, Per, *elskling*,' she whispered, then, translating the word into English, 'darling'.

There was a deep, delighted laugh from the other end and then silence.

Kirsten returned next morning at coffee time. She carried in the tray, saying she had met Fru Vatne on the way, and Fru Vatne had provided another cup so that they could share the coffee.

As Noelle poured, Kirsten said, 'So I now owe my brother money?' When Noelle looked at her inquiringly, she went on, 'He has without doubt won his bet. You spent the night with him in his log cabin.'

'Yes, but not in the way you think, Kirsten.'

Kirsten laughed unbelievingly. 'I know my brother too well for that. I heard on the grapevine how he kissed you good-bye when he went off, and phoned you last night. No man shows that concern for nothing.'

For the first time, Noelle found her friend's bluntness grating. But why? she asked herself agonizingly. Because it devalued her relationship with Per? Made it seem sordid and commonplace, a surreptitious little affair between an employee and her boss?

'He—' she began, but she had to stop. 'He loves me,' she was going to say. But how did she know? He had never told her, not once in the weeks she had known him, despite his kisses. Not once in their hours together in the cabin, despite his lovemaking, had he told her he loved her.

'Loves you?' Kirsten said with a laugh in her voice. She shook her head. 'He did it to win his bet.'

Noelle went cold. 'What do you mean?'

'I mean that when I bet him he wouldn't succeed in making you one of his women he said, "I shall have her eating out of the palm of my hand before her time here with us is over."'

Eating out of the palm of his hand! 'But,' Noelle protested, realizing how stupid she must sound, 'I didn't hear him say that.'

'Of course you didn't. We conversed in our own language. You don't think he would have allowed you to hear that, do you? You'd have known what he was up to from the start!'

Noelle heard again their conversation on the telephone. *Admit you're my woman*, he had said, *admit it!* Yes, she had answered eagerly, *yes, yes, yes*!

No wonder he had laughed with such pleasure and triumph. Wasn't that his moment of victory, the culmination of all his efforts?

The arrogance of the man made her burn. Her inability to

hit back because of his absence brought tears of frustration to her eyes.

Kirsten asked casually, 'Upset? If you are, I'm sorry, Noelle, but you should never have taken my brother seriously. I've warned you against him so often. And there's Sonja, don't forget.'

Forget Sonja? How could she? Yet in her foolish self-deception that Per's feelings for her were deep and sincere, hadn't she done just that?

'Upset?' she said to Kirsten, pretending indifference. 'Your brother means nothing to me, so how could I be upset? He's fun to be with, but beyond that he leaves me cold. Now Einar,' she made herself sigh, 'he really was something. I'm glad he gave me his address.'

'North Cape is a long way north,' Kirsten warned. 'But I know how you feel. He was quite a guy, that boy. If he hadn't been yours, I would have made a try for him myself. What will you do? When you finish here, will you go up to him where he lives?'

Noelle forced a dreamy smile. 'Just try to stop me!'

Kirsten laughed. 'Thank heaven for that! I really began to think you had fallen for my brother, after all. The money's mine! Wait till I tell him how much he owes me. And I've been proved right – his charm is not foolproof, as he claims.' At the door she said, 'You're quite a girl under all that reserve, aren't you? You spent one, if not two nights with Einar—' Noelle checked her protest just in time, 'and a night with my brother. And there was I saying how pure your morals were!'

As she went out she laughed, and the laughter echoed up and down the corridor. It sounded long after she had gone, but in reality it rang only in Noelle's ears, mocking her and making her cover them to try to shut it out.

CHAPTER TEN

THE engines of the ship were throbbing under the passengers' feet. Bergen was behind them and they were making their way through the multitude of islands scattered around the coast.

Noelle's journey had begun just before lunch, when she had left the hotel, rucksack on her back, and had caught the bus to the railway station at Voss, an hour's drive away. The train had taken her to Bergen and she had boarded the ship with only half an hour to spare. Because she had not booked in advance, she had had to accept whatever accommodation they could offer. She was sharing a cabin with three other girls.

Noelle did not care where she slept because she knew that, however comfortable her bed – and the bunk bed she would be sleeping in would not be particularly comfortable – she would not sleep. Her mind was numb and she was in a state of shock, although, as she kept telling herself, she could not understand why. What had she really expected from her relationship with Per? Had she sincerely believed he would tell her he loved her and that he would continue to love her, and no other, until the end of his days?

Since she had spent those hours with him in his log cabin, she had been living in a dream world. When Kirsten had turned that dream into a nightmare, her only desire had been to run away as fast and as far as she possibly could from the Arneson family.

She had left two notes behind in her – Per's – room. One had been for Fru Vatne, thanking her for her kindness and telling her she was going home. Her mother would look after her and attend to her cuts and bruises, she said. The other note had been addressed to Kirsten.

'I'm sorry to leave without seeing you,' the note said, 'but as I told you, I want to see Einar again so much I'm travelling north before the summer is over and Einar returns to college. I know you will understand. I shall be in touch with you some time in the future. Thank you and your brother for all you have done for me. With much affection, Noelle.'

Noelle rested against the rail and watched Bergen with its backdrop of mountains recede into the mist. She was saying good-bye to Norway and she was crying inside. Like the troll in the story, she had stayed too long in the open and had been caught by the sunlight. And although she had turned and fled, she had not run fast enough. The troll in the legend had left his foot behind and it had solidified into rock. She, Noelle, had left behind her heart and it, too, had turned to stone. Her heart was in Norway, and there it would remain for ever.

Her fingers felt in her pocket for Per's troll. She had brought it with her simply because she could not bear to leave it behind. But the sweater Per had given her lay folded on a shelf in the wardrobe.

There was nothing more to do now but wait for the journey across the North Sea to be over, and then she would travel to her parents' home in Wiltshire. She would find herself a job and she would try to forget.

Few passengers were outside. There was an autumnal feeling in the air and they had sought the warmth of the lounge. Noelle preferred the peace and quiet of the almost deserted deck, although she had to turn up her collar to keep out the cool breeze. The sea was as grey and restless as her state of mind and it was a strange kind of comfort to stare into its depths and feel herself at one with its mood.

To her surprise, she did sleep that night, but she awoke almost as exhausted as when she had settled down. Her body may have rested, but her dreams had been disturbed. After breakfast she drifted on to the deck again, avoiding anyone who looked as though they might speak to her.

At midday the ship docked at the quay in Newcastle. Noelle shouldered her rucksack and walked with the crowd down the gangway. She noticed it was raining and told herself sourly that the weather suited her mood. Customs did not detain her and she passed through quickly. The pelting rain made her hesitate for a few moments, but she put up her hood, pushed her hands deep into the pockets of her jacket and with her rucksack weighing her down, stepped out into the rain.

She had not gone more than a few paces when her arm was seized in a grip like a vice and she was swung to a halt. Momentarily frightened, she stared at the man who had brought her round to face him. Her cheeks drained of colour, her throat went dry and her breath stayed where it was – in her lungs.

'Per!' she gasped. 'Why—?'

The pressure of his arm began to hurt and she tried to pull away from him. His reaction was to tighten his hold.

'I've got a bus to catch, so let me go, please,' she said. 'It goes to the city centre and if I miss it I'll have to wait a long time for the next.'

'You're coming with me in the car.'

'I'm not. You can't make me. Let me go, Per. We've got nothing to say to each other—'

'On the contrary, I have a great deal to say to *you*.' He forced her to walk beside him. 'I'm going to the city centre, too – to the hotel where I've booked a room. And you're coming with me. Give me that rucksack.' She started to walk on, but he barred her way, slipping the straps from her shoulders and lifting the rucksack off her back.

He unlocked the passenger door of the car and almost bundled her in.

'You're abducting me,' she said plaintively. 'It's against the law.'

'Call it what you like, but whatever it is, there's not a damned thing you can do about it.'

He spun the steering wheel, swinging the car away from the quay and on to the road. There was silence for a long time, a sulky silence on her part and a tight-lipped one on his.

Noelle could not bear it, so she asked ungraciously, 'Is this your car?'

'No. I hired it.'

'How – how did you arrive in England before I did?'

'I came by plane.'

'How did you know where to find me?'

'Kirsten phoned to tell me I had lost my bet and to gloat over the fact. In the course of our somewhat acid conversation she told me you had gone and had left two notes, each telling a different story. She said hers was the correct one, but I guessed the one you wrote to Fru Vatne was nearer the truth. I took a chance, caught the first available flight from the airport near my uncle's home and arrived here this morning. Now tell me *your* story. And,' his lips tightened, 'it had better be good!'

'So I mean nothing to you? So I leave you cold?' Per stood by the window of the hotel bedroom, leaning against the sill, his eyes cool and watchful. The daylight outside made his shape into a dark silhouette. It was threatening and totally inscrutable.

Noelle looked at him, startled and a little dazed. She had heard those words somewhere . . .

'That's what you told Kirsten, isn't it?'

Now she remembered. Of course Kirsten would have told her brother what she had said about him, if only to prove, as she thought, how immune her best friend was to his charms. Noelle could only nod, because it was true. 'But I said them to—' To mislead you. But she did not speak the words.

'To what?'

Noelle glanced round, scarcely taking in the luxury of the room, the soft camel carpet, the polished furniture, the door to the bathroom, the deep red quilt and cover on the bed.

'Hadn't you better start explaining?'

'I'm tired, Per.' Her glance held appeal, and her fingers

strayed to the plaster at her temple. 'I still haven't fully recovered from that fall.' He frowned, not with sympathy but with a touch of anger. Noelle moved a few paces and sat on the bed.

He said curtly, 'I gave Fru Vatne strict instructions to look after you personally and tend your injuries. I should have told her to turn the key every time she left you.'

'She did look after me, very well. It was not her fault that I–'

'Ran away? Well, tell me why you did. Something fairly drastic must have precipitated your flight from Norway. Did someone say something to upset you? Was it Sonja?'

'I haven't seen Sonja.'

'Then it must have been Kirsten. Is that right?'

After a pause she looked up imploringly. 'I told you, I'm tired, Per. And hungry. Let me go, please.'

'I shall let you rest – and eat – when I've finished with you.'

'You've wasted your time and your money coming after me.'

'That's my business. I'm determined to get an explanation out of you, even if it takes all day and,' softly, eyeing the bed, 'all night.'

She said wearily, 'What do you want to know?'

'I want to know why, after almost admitting on the phone that you loved me, you should put the width of the North Sea between us the following day.'

'Told you I loved you?' She was roused now. 'I merely said "Darling". And,' bitterly, 'what does a woman calling you "darling" mean to you? You have so many at your beck and call. Not content with Sonja, you have to have me tagging along, too.'

She stood up. Now she had started, she would not stop. 'That first day on the ship you called women unscrupulous. All they wanted, you said, was to find the richest man of their acquaintance and fasten their claws into him, demanding marriage and a home. Well, where I'm concerned, you were wrong, utterly wrong. All right,' with a catch in her voice, 'like other women you know, I might have stretched out my arms to you – once – at the cabin in the mountains. But now I've closed them again. And the sooner you absorb that into your system, the better for us both.'

She picked up her rucksack and made for the door, but he was there first, turning the key and pocketing it.

Noelle looked round wildly. 'I'll press that bell, I'll get one of the staff up here.'

Eyes narrow, Per said, 'You won't threaten me, my girl. I'll put you across my knee first. Well, have you finished?'

'No. You had a bet with Kirsten about me.'

'So what if I did?'

Noelle drew a long breath, held it a moment, then said, 'Part of that bet was to prove that your charm, when you exercised it on a woman, any woman, was infallible. The other part was,' she paused because it was painful even to admit to herself that he had in fact achieved his objective, 'that before my time with you was up, you would have me "eating out of the palm of your hand". That, if you must know, was the precipitating factor that made me leave Norway so quickly. I couldn't even bear to be in the same country as you, let alone the same room. Now you have the truth, let me go.'

If he did not relent and open the door at once, she knew she would have no more strength to draw on and would have to sink down on that bed again.

But he did not relent. He approached her slowly and she backed away, blurting out, more on the defensive than ever, 'At the cabin you said you had tamed me. Well, once again you were wrong. No man will ever tame me, do you hear?' He went on walking towards her and she felt despair at her inability to deflect him from his purpose – it was there in his tensed muscles and taut jawline – of manhandling her.

'Not even you,' she added, then more aggressively to cover her anxiety, '*certainly* not you!'

'No?'

She realized at last how useless her efforts were to weaken his determination. She stood still, her heart hammering, helplessly awaiting his next move. It was not long in coming. He took the rucksack from her shoulder, peeled the jacket from her arms and flung it on a chair.

Then his arms were around her and his mouth was punishing hers with a kiss which took the life and breath from her body. He did not leave her with enough strength to make even a token resistance to his display of masculine power. His kisses moved over her face, her throat, and pushing aside her sleeveless top, her shoulder. His hands were not idle and were compelling her slowly, expertly into a whimpering, total surrender.

He brought tears to her eyes, but he disregarded them. Not until he drew from her, out of her depths, words that he was resolutely determined to tear from her, did his grip upon her body loosen a mere fraction.

'I love you, Per,' she whispered, hiding her face against him, 'oh, I love you so . . .'

Noelle did not care now how much she had told him. Whether or not he loved her was at that moment irrelevant. She loved him so completely she would do anything, anything he asked of her. This she told him in her actions, the way her eyes sought his, gazing into them with adoration, the way she clung and pulled down his head, so that her mouth could rest against his.

'I'm sorry, Per,' she sobbed, 'I can't help it.'

'Carry on, *min elskede*, my darling. You're delighting me. Carry on, *min kjæreste lille skatt*, my dearest little treasure! Of course I had that bet with Kirsten. And why? Because from our first meeting I was determined to make you mine. Even when you defied me as you so often did, even when I found you in Einar Olsen's room and I was so bitterly jealous I dismissed you from the staff and only Olaf Krüger's pleading saved you—'

'Would you have let me go?'

'Only as far as my room which you occupied in the staff

house. I would have relented at once and given you another job. There were plenty you could have done, in the office, at reception, even bed-making.'

'But, Per,' they were holding each other, sitting side by side on the bed, 'you were so angry with me.'

'And why, *kjæreste*? Because not only was I jealous, but as you stood there defying me, you seemed to hate me so. The one woman I really wanted to like me, love me, and there she was challenging me, white-faced and full of dislike.' She shook her head. 'Or so it seemed. Tell me, did you love me then?'

She nodded. 'I think it happened right at the start, on board ship. I felt the love increasing inside me until it went into every corner of my body!'

He kissed her lingeringly, then, 'Einar Olsen?' He held her away, looking into her face.

'I told you the truth, Per. He did his best and,' with a smile, 'it was a good best, but he didn't succeed.'

'Your shadow, the young English boy?'

'Poor Mark! He was sweet and I was sorry for him, but – Per, it was you, all the time.'

'And you didn't tell me! The time we've wasted, beloved.'

She rearranged his tie. 'Per, I—' He looked at her questioningly. 'I – quite understand if—' she took a breath, 'if you don't love me.'

He exploded, first with disbelief, then with anger. 'Don't *love* you? What do you think this is all about? What sort of a heel do you think I am? What kind of relationship do you think I'm asking of you?'

Her fingers stilled his lips. 'You haven't told me, Per.'

'But surely you could see it in my every action, every kiss I gave you, in how much I wanted you in the cabin, but restrained myself because I knew you didn't want it that way. *Elskling*, even if you hadn't fallen down that stairway and hurt yourself, I would have held back unless you had shown any sign of wanting me as I wanted you. But you would like me to put it into words, so now I shall tell you. Now I shall say in my own language – I shall teach you Norwegian one day, sweetheart – *jeg elsker deg . . .* I love you. *Vil du gifte deg med meg? Vil du bli min kone?* Will you marry me? Will you be my wife?' Softly, tenderly, '*Vil du bli min hustru?* Will you bear my children and look after my home? What more can I say to persuade you I love you? Well, my darling?'

She took a breath and looked up at him. '*Ja,* Per. Did I say it right?'

'*Min elskede,*' he was laughing, 'the accent was perfect! I shall make a linguist of you yet.'

'Sonja?' she whispered.

'Sonja ceased to exist for me the day you came into my life. You believe that, my love?'

'Yes, Per. Per?' He lifted her face and brushed her lips with his. 'Will you go back to Norway now?'

'And let you out of my sight? I shall return to Norway when we are married. Today we spend together. I shall book a room for you here. Tomorrow we drive across the country to your parents' house. There I shall be the perfect son-in-law-to-be and inform your father of my intentions. Then, in a day or so, we shall marry. Or do you want a big wedding, with lots of people—?'

'No. Only my parents. And yours?'

He nodded. 'They will fly here.'

'And Kirsten, if she can get here in time.'

'She will,' said Per.

'And,' Noelle went on with an impudent smile, 'you, of course.'

He spanked her lightly, then he whispered, 'Shall I tell you something? I have a picture of you in my wallet that I've been carrying around with me for weeks. The photograph Kirsten took of you in Norwegian bridal dress. That day you looked so beautiful, so irresistible, I nearly asked you to marry me then.'

She put her hand into her pocket. 'And here's the troll you

gave me. On the ship I kept touching it and stroking it and wishing it would bring me the luck you said it would.'

'Ah,' he said, smiling knowingly, 'then I have him, that little troll, to thank for all my happiness now. You know why I gave him to you? As a child I loved him. Now, as a man, I love you. So I gave him to the woman I loved. If only I could have taught him to speak, he could have passed the message on!'

Noelle thought, as he kissed her again, My heart has been restored to my body. It's no longer made of stone, fixed for ever in the mountains of Norway. My heart was caught in the sunlight, but unlike the troll's foot, the sun warmed it and brought it back to life.

Per murmured, his mouth against hers, 'You're all I ever wanted in a woman. You have spirit and intelligence. And,' with a teasing smile, 'you are tractable and docile, but it is spiced with indignation and a touch of anger. But above all, you have warmth and, as I know from experience, passion. Tell me, my darling, what was it that you wanted in me,' his smile teased again, 'my money?'

'No, only yourself,' she sighed contentedly, snuggling into his arms. 'And your love.'